After

"Ben? Lissa, Ben and I broke up. Didn't you know that?"

Something lifted inside of me. "You and Ben broke up? What happened?"

"He got drunk at Terri Anderson's party. Started dancing around in this hideous robe he found in her mom's closet. And then he ended up in a corner with Alice Spradling. End of story."

"What—they were fooling around?"

"Yep."

I stared at my jeans. The lightness I'd felt was gone. "Funny how that happens, huh? Get drunk, fool around . . . end of story."

"What are you talking about, Lissa?"

I gripped the phone. I couldn't believe I'd said that, and now I didn't know how to take it back. And part of me didn't want to take it back, wanted Kate to hear it and respond and . . . and just *talk* to me about it.

"I thought we decided not to fight anymore," Kate said. Her voice was cool.

"I'm not fighting. I just . . . I think we need to talk."

"About what? There's nothing to talk about."

"Kate, come on." My heart pounded. "That night? At Rob's house?"

There was a long silence.

"We were drunk," Kate finally said.

"You were. I wasn't."

OTHER SPEAK BOOKS

Catalyst	Laurie Halse Anderson
Empress of the World	Sara Ryan
Fat Kid Rules the World	K. L. Going
My Heartbeat	Garret Freymann-Weyr
Postcards from No Man's Land	Aidan Chambers
Pretty Things	Sara Manning
Someone Like You	Sarah Dessen

Kissing Kate

Lauren Myracle

speak

An Imprint of Penguin Group (USA) Inc.

SPEAK

Published by the Penguin Group

Penguin Group (USA) Inc., 345 Hudson Street, New York, New York 10014, U.S.A.
Penguin Group (Canada), 90 Eglinton Avenue East, Suite 700, Toronto,
Ontario, Canada M4P 2Y3 (a division of Pearson Penguin Canada Inc.)
Penguin Books Ltd, 80 Strand, London WC2R 0RL, England
Penguin Ireland, 25 St Stephen's Green, Dublin 2, Ireland (a division of Penguin Books Ltd)
Penguin Group (Australia), 250 Camberwell Road, Camberwell, Victoria 3124, Australia
(a division of Pearson Australia Group Pty Ltd)
Penguin Books India Pvt Ltd, 11 Community Centre,
Panchsheel Park, New Delhi - 110 017, India
Penguin Group (NZ), 67 Apollo Drive, Mairangi Bay, Auckland 1311, New Zealand
(a division of Pearson New Zealand Ltd)
Penguin Books (South Africa) (Pty) Ltd, 24 Sturdee Avenue,
Rosebank, Johannesburg 2196, South Africa

Registered Offices: Penguin Books Ltd, 80 Strand, London WC2R 0RL, England

First published in the United States of America by Dutton Books,
a member of Penguin Putnam Inc., 2003
Published by Speak, an imprint of Penguin Group (USA) Inc., 2004

This edition published by Speak, an imprint of Penguin Group (USA) Inc., 2007

3 5 7 9 10 8 6 4 2

Copyright © Lauren Myracle, 2003
All rights reserved

The excerpts and references on pages 25, 26, 45, 47, and 74 are from
Lucid Dreaming: The Power of Being Awake and Aware in Your Dreams,
by Stephen LaBerge, Ph.D., published by Ballantine Books, New York.

THE LIBRARY OF CONGRESS HAS CATALOGED THE DUTTON EDITION AS FOLLOWS:
Myracle, Lauren, date.
Kissing Kate / by Lauren Myracle.
p.   cm.
Summary: Sixteen-year-old Lissa's relationship with her best friend changes
after they kiss at a party and Lissa does not know what to do,
until she gets help from an unexpected new friend.
ISBN: 0-525-46917-6 (hc)
[1. Friendship—Fiction. 2. Lesbians—Fiction. 3. Homosexuality—Fiction.
4. Identity—Fiction.] I. Title.
PZ7.M9955 Ki 2003   [Fic]—dc21   2002074145

Speak ISBN 978-0-14-240869-8

Designed by Heather Wood

Printed in the United States of America

Except in the United States of America, this book is sold subject to the condition that
it shall not, by way of trade or otherwise, be lent, re-sold, hired out, or otherwise
circulated without the publisher's prior consent in any form of binding or cover
other than that in which it is published and without a similar condition
including this condition being imposed on the subsequent purchaser.

The publisher does not have any control over and does not assume any
responsibility for author or third-party Web sites or their content.

FOR JACK, WHO FLIES ME THROUGH KISSES

*Thanks to the following, whose encouragement and response helped shape the book:
Brock Cole, Sharron Darrow, Karen Hollenbeck-Wuest, Shawna Jackson, Jill Greene,
Christine Kechter, Tom Kechter, Chuck Kechter, Jackie Owens, Julianne Sanders,
Maggie Adams, Virginia MacKinnon, and the faculty and students of Vermont
College's graduate program in writing for children and young adults.*

*I especially thank my dear friend Laura Pritchett, who talks to me about writing and
children, children and writing. Her example gives me strength.*

*I am grateful to my family for their steady and loving support: my mother, Ruth
White, for never suggesting I choose a more practical career; my fathers, Tim White
and Don Myracle, for, respectively, helping me navigate the streets of Atlanta and
encouraging an early love of books; and my sister, Susan White, for inspiring me,
advising me, and making me laugh.*

*A thousand thanks to my editor, Susan Van Metre, who is amazing beyond words.
Thanks, too, to her assistants, Susan Finch and Caroline Beltz.*

And finally I thank my husband, Jack Martin, who makes it all possible.

Kissing Kate

CHAPTER 1

IT WAS TINY, NO MORE THAN A LINE of blood bubbling up at the base of my finger, but the knife clattered to the counter and I sank to the floor, sucking my hand and crying as if I were six years old instead of sixteen. The linoleum was ugly, and I could see dust and crumbs scattered beneath the cabinets, and it occurred to me that if this was how I was going to feel for the rest of my life, if slicing a bagel could bring me to tears, then I'd have been better off not knowing Kate at all. And then my head grew light, because how could I even think such a thing?

I take it back, I prayed. I squeezed my eyes shut and wished I could take it all back, everything that had happened, so that Kate and I could return to being friends like we used to be. I felt wrong inside without her, weepy and miserable and pathetic. And that was the part I didn't get, because didn't she feel that way, too?

We'd been best friends since we were twelve, long enough that our names were paired in everyone's minds: Kate and Lissa. Always her name first, not that I cared. If anything, I still felt surprised we'd been linked at all, that she'd picked me when she could have chosen anyone. Although really, it was our seventh-grade gym teacher who did the choosing.

"What was that teacher's name?" Kate asked just last month. "The one whose P.E. class we were in, the one who assigned us to be partners?"

Kate couldn't call it up, but I remembered exactly. It was Mrs. Klause. I remembered everything about that day, even its lousy start. I was running late because I couldn't find a permission slip I was supposed to turn in, and on top of that, my Uncle Jerry picked that morning to cough and tug on his ear before finally suggesting that perhaps I should wash my new bra since I'd worn it for a week straight and didn't I think maybe . . . ? Only he didn't call it a "bra," he called it an "upper undergarment," and he about died getting those words out. We both did. I'd bought the bra on my own, which meant that Jerry must have noticed the outline of the straps beneath my T-shirts or felt them on one of the rare occasions when he gave me a hug. For him to mention it at all was astounding.

I swear, I think back on Jerry during moments like that and I'm amazed he's survived as well as he has. That we all have. Jerry moved in with us when I was eight, after my parents were killed in a plane crash, and he's been taking care of me and my little sister, Beth, ever since. It hasn't been easy.

Anyway, I'm sure he didn't mean I should wash it right then. His worried eyes said as much when I dropped my books and fled back up to my room. But he was right about how long it had been, and my first class was P.E., which meant changing into my P.E. uniform. I'd avoided putting my bra in the laundry hamper out of normal, twelve-year-old embarrassment. (Jerry did the wash, and I didn't want him running across it.) But the thought of the girls in the locker room smirking as I pulled off my shirt was a million times worse.

I washed my bra in the sink, then blew it dry with my hair dryer. By the time Jerry dropped me off at school, it was 8:15, and I had to go to the office for a late pass.

"Better hurry," the secretary said. I grabbed the pass and ran to the gym. I had the locker room all to myself—wouldn't you know it—and I changed in record time and dashed to the basketball court, where Mrs. Klause had already unrolled the cushiony, blue floor mat. The other girls sat in a circle at her feet, and their heads swiveled my way as I darted across the floor. Mrs. Klause gave me a disapproving stare, then continued with her instructions. "You'll need to master the headstand, handstand, and arabesque for our unit on balance," she said. "Today, we start with the headstand."

She squatted, then placed her hands and head on the floor and tipped her lower body above her hips, first resting her knees on her elbows and then straightening her legs into the air. Her gym shorts bunched around her bottom, making some of the girls snicker. She lowered her legs and stood up.

"That is the correct position for a headstand: knees locked, toes pointed, no swaying back and forth. Any questions?" She scanned the circle, daring anyone else to laugh. "Good. Amy, why don't you work with Elizabeth; Karena, work with Maggie; Jody, you work with Rebecca—"

I drew my knees to my chest and wrapped my arms around my shins. I hated it when she made us work with partners. I was neither cute nor outgoing, and most of the girls groaned when they were paired with me. During our unit on calisthenics, I'd been assigned to work with Callie Roberts, who begged me to go to Mrs. Klause and ask to be switched. I wouldn't, and Callie marked me down as having done only ten jumping jacks when really I'd done twenty-five.

"And Kate, let's see, why don't you work with"—her eyes landed on me—"Lissa."

I ducked my head, resting my chin on my kneecaps. Kate was small and blond and pretty, and she had a laugh like an open present. Compared to me, she was a goddess. Plus, she was a gymnast. I'd seen her practicing after school. She wouldn't want to work with me. She'd think I was a big, dark clod.

Mrs. Klause clapped her hands. "All right, girls. Get to work!"

I stayed where I was. A pair of sneakers entered my line of vision, and I lifted my head to see Kate gazing down at me.

"Ready?" she said.

"You already know how to do a headstand," I said.

She shrugged. "Do you?"

"I know *how*—I just can't do it. But you don't have to help me."

"I don't mind." She knelt beside me. "Try one, and I'll watch."

Great, I thought, *I'll fall on my butt and you can watch.* But she was looking at me with her wide blue eyes, and if she was being mean, she was doing a great job of hiding it. I got on my knees and put my head on the mat, but when I tried to lift my lower body, I tipped forward and rolled onto my back.

"I feel like a bug," I said, staring up at the high ceiling.

Kate smiled. "Try again."

This time I got my knees onto my elbows before teetering sideways and landing in a heap.

Kate covered her mouth with her hand. "Whoops."

"You do one," I said.

She put her head on the mat and pushed herself up, extending her legs and pointing her toes in the air. She stayed like that for a couple of seconds before bending her knees and rolling forward in a somersault. "I think it's the way I put my hands," she said. "I think you're putting yours too far apart."

I put my hands closer together, but I still tipped over. "I can't do it."

"Yes, you can. Put your hands on the floor, okay?"

I did as I was told.

"See how your fingers are pointing straight out? You want them to point more to the middle, like this." She adjusted my hands with her own, angling my fingers inward. I thought of the way her spine straightened as she did her headstand, and I wondered how it felt to be so lovely.

My cut had almost stopped bleeding, and I made myself go to the bathroom for a Band-Aid. I washed my hand, then tore off a piece of toilet paper and pressed it against my finger. A small red dot soaked through, and my tears welled up all over again. Such a dumb thing, a cut on my finger, and yet here I was sniveling like there was no tomorrow.

Kate would never fall apart like this. Even in seventh grade, she'd been sure of herself. How could she not be? At school she roamed the halls with the cheerleaders and the members of the pep squad, and during lunch she ate with the most popular kids. Until that gym class, I'd never spoken to her, not really. That's why I was so startled when she came up to me after school that day. I was sitting on the curb near the faculty parking lot, waiting for Jerry to pick me up, when out of nowhere Kate plopped down beside me.

"Hi," she said.

"Uh, hi," I said. I glanced around, but there was no one else nearby. "What's up?"

"Not much. Just killing time before gymnastics practice." She leaned back on her elbows and crossed her feet on the asphalt. "Coach Greer has a meeting, so we're starting late."

I nodded. She wore a thin silver bracelet on her left arm, and it glinted in the sun. Her wrists were tiny.

"Does your head still hurt?" she asked.

It took me a moment to get what she was talking about. Then I remembered: the headstands.

"Only if I press it on the ground and put all my weight on it," I said. I made a face. "Which, you know, I like to do a lot."

She laughed. "You did get better, though. You almost had it those last couple of times."

"Yeah, because my head was dented in by then. By the end of the unit, I'll be like Barney Rubble, with a big, square head." I imitated her position, leaning back on my elbows so that the concrete dug into my skin. "It must be fun to be good at that stuff—headstands and cartwheels and all that."

"I guess." She glanced at me. "What about you? What do you do?"

"What do you mean, what do I do?"

"You know, what are you good at?" She said it so easily, like *everyone* was good at something. But I wasn't on any teams, and in P.E. I was one of the last people picked, even for something simple like dodgeball. I didn't play the piano. I didn't draw. What did I do?

Karen and Elise, two girls from our grade, came around the corner of the school. They stopped when they saw us, and their eyebrows went up.

"Hi, Kate," Elise said. "Hi, Lissa." She turned back to Kate. "We're going to walk over to Dairy Queen and get a Blizzard. Want to come?"

I focused on the pavement. The lines marking the parking spaces were faint and needed to be repainted.

"Nah," Kate said. "Y'all go on. I'll see you in practice."

"You sure?" Elise's eyes flicked to me. "Well, whatever." She nudged Karen and they walked away. Karen said something in a low voice, and the two of them broke out laughing.

"Why didn't you go with them?" I said. It came out sounding snotty, and I blushed. I sat up and wrapped my arms around my legs.

"I don't know," Kate said. "I'm not hungry. And Elise can be kind of a pain sometimes. Anyway, I know both of them already."

I sat still, feeling the sun on my neck. I wanted to say something witty, something to prove I was worth getting to know, but the words wouldn't come. I felt that way a lot, like I had thoughts within me but it took a long time for them to bubble to the surface. By that point, most people had lost interest.

"You never told me what you like to do," Kate said.

"That's because I can't think of anything."

She rolled her eyes.

"I'm serious. I can't."

She looked at me, then gave a funny half-smile. "I bet you're good at tons of things. You're just being modest."

That's when I felt it. It was her expression more than anything, as if she'd summed me up and actually liked what she saw. But that was four years ago. Now when Kate looked at me, which didn't happen very often, something in her eyes wouldn't let me past.

I asked her once why she had come up to me that day, why she had decided to be so nice.

"Oh, you know," she teased. "I was bored, I had nothing else to do—"

"Come on," I said. This was when we were still friends, so I grinned and shoved her shoulder.

"Well," she said, "part of it was that you seemed so solemn, like you had some great secret or something. But you were funny, too. You made me laugh." She looked at me, one of those penetrating gazes that made me feel special. "You were different from what I expected."

"Oh, great," I said.

"In a good way, Lissa. You know that."

But I didn't, not anymore. Not since two weeks ago in Rob's gazebo, when Kate leaned in to kiss me and like an idiot I kissed her back. All I knew now was that nothing lasted forever, even a friendship, and that being "different" felt the same as being alone.

CHAPTER 2

"BETH!" I CALLED. "BREAKFAST!" I felt conspicuous with my bandaged finger, but at least I'd stopped crying. I passed Jerry his bagel, then plucked Beth's from the toaster and dropped it on a plate.

"Thanks," Jerry said. He put down the paper.

"You going in today?" I asked. Jerry used to work the grave-yard shift at the city waste-treatment facility, but he gave that up, along with his trailer and his vintage Harley-Davidson, when he came to live with us. Now he managed a plant nurs-ery over by Chastain Park, and he often worked on weekends.

"Yeah. Sophie's trying her hand at the cash register, so I need to be there to supervise. You want to come? Got some new saplings that need to be potted."

"Can't. I'm getting my hair cut." I craned my head toward the door. "Be-*eth!*"

She pounded down the stairs and dropped into her seat.

She reached for the jar of jam. "Hey, Lissa," she said, "I want to go to the mall with Nikki. Can you drop us off?"

"I guess," I said. "But we need to leave soon."

"Okay. Nikki's cousin Vanessa might come, too. She just moved here from North Carolina, and she's going to be in my homeroom at school."

"Well, you be nice to her," Jerry said. He took a sip of coffee. "I'm sure she'd appreciate a friend."

"Nikki says she was the most popular girl in her class where she used to live. She has a tattoo."

"A tattoo?"

"Uh-huh, a daisy. I'm going to get one, too."

"Beth—" Jerry said. He turned to me for help.

"They come in a package for about two bucks," I said. "You press them onto your skin and they wash off after a couple of days. They're like stickers."

"They're not like *stickers*," Beth said. "Anyway, when I'm older I'm going to get a real one, like Kate's."

Jerry lowered his cup. "Kate has a tattoo? A real one?"

I glared at Beth. "No."

"She does so. On her ankle, a little purple moon."

I could feel Jerry's look, but I didn't respond.

Too late, Beth realized she'd messed up. "Oh. But maybe that was someone else. I think I got confused."

I ignored her. By now my bagel was cold, and I pushed it away. "So Sophie's working out?" I asked Jerry.

His brow cleared. "Yeah. So far, so good. She's a chatterbox, though—I'll tell you that."

Sophie was Jerry's new floor clerk, and she was nice in a goofy, overbearing kind of way. She had to be in her late thirties, yet she still wore ceramic earrings shaped like cats and hearts and question marks, and her tennis shoes were red with sparkly gold laces. And Jerry was right: she was definitely a talker. The day I met her she went on for twenty minutes about her gray-and-white-striped kitten, which she'd rescued from the pound the week before. "I named him Q.T.," she told me. "As in the initials." She waited for me to get it. "Q.T., because he's such a cutie pie. Isn't that a hoot?"

"Well, good," I said now. "You need someone to make the customers feel welcome."

"Maybe." He downed the last of his coffee. "So how *is* Kate? She hasn't been around much these days."

I took my dishes to the sink. "She's been busy."

"Busy? I thought you two were glued together at the hip."

"She's got her gymnastics meets. You know. And school's been kind of overwhelming, even though the semester just started. Fall semester, junior year—it's when all the teachers start piling on the work. They say it's to get us ready for college. Anyway, it's just been really busy for everyone."

"Huh," Jerry said. "Sounds like it." He pushed his chair out from the table and returned to his paper.

Beth brought up her plate and rinsed it off. "Maybe you could ask her to go with us to the mall," she said softly.

"No."

"But—"

"I said no, Beth." I yanked open the dishwasher. "Go call Nikki. If she's going with you, she needs to get ready. I'm leaving in half an hour."

Upstairs in my room, I flopped onto my bed and stared at the ceiling. Why had I treated Beth like such a jerk for mentioning Kate's tattoo? It wasn't my job to protect Kate, and even if it were, she hardly needed protection from Jerry. It wasn't like he was going to call her parents or anything. Anyway, it had been almost a month since she'd gotten it. Surely they'd noticed by now.

"A *tattoo*?" I'd exclaimed when Kate first suggested it. We were sitting in a booth at McDonald's, and I looked at her over the top of my Coke. "Kate."

"What's wrong with a tattoo? I'll get a cute one, not 'I Love Mother' stenciled across my biceps." She laughed. "God, wouldn't she love that."

I'd smiled. Kate's mom already hated the fact that we didn't dress more like "ladies." "You two have such darling figures," she chided. "You need to accentuate them. Boys like to see a girl's curves."

"You have to come with me or I'll wimp out," Kate said, slapping some money on the table and standing up. "I *need* you, Lissa."

At the tattoo parlor—"Tattoo U" it was called—Kate got nervous and clutched my arm. "What if it hurts?" she whispered as a man named Big Joe readied the needle.

"What if you get gangrene?" I whispered back.

She drove her elbow into my side.

"Ready?" said Big Joe. He wore a cracked leather jacket, and he had thick lines of oil, or maybe dye, under his fingernails. His stomach hung over his jeans like a sack of flour.

Kate sat down across from him. "It won't hurt, will it?"

"Hell, no. No more'n a bee sting. You ever been stung by a bee?"

Kate nodded.

Big Joe cackled. "Hurts, don't it?"

Kate's eyes flew to me, and I lifted my shoulders.

Big Joe had her prop her ankle on a stool so he could stencil the outline of the tattoo. "A snake, right? Heh. Just kidding." He switched on the tattoo machine, Kate turned pale, and fifteen minutes later it was done. Big Joe taped a gauze pad over Kate's ankle and wiped his hands on his jeans.

"Leave this bandage on till the next time you take a shower," he instructed. "Then turn the water up hot—hot as you can stand it—and let the bandage soak off. The hot water'll soak the plasma out of your skin, too, make it heal up quicker." He gave her a tube of antibiotic. "You'll want to smear on some of this ointment every day for two to three days. After that, switch to plain lotion. No aloe vera or any of that scented crap. Any questions?"

Kate stood up. She was still a little shaky, but the color was coming back to her cheeks. "How long will it take to heal?"

"Two to three weeks, unless I screwed up." He slapped his leg. "That'll be forty dollars, no out-of-state checks."

Afterward, we went to Baskin-Robbins to celebrate. "You're amazing," I told Kate as she slid in beside me in the booth.

"I thought I was going to faint. I didn't know it would bleed so much. Did you?"

I shook my head. "I guess I thought it was more like getting your ears pierced."

"Yeah. Remind me to put on socks when I go home, so Mom won't see the bandage."

I slurped my milk shake. "So. What about Big Joe? Pretty hot, huh?"

"Omigod. Did you see that he does body piercings, too?"

"You're tempted, aren't you?"

She snorted, then leaned against me and put her head on my shoulder. "Hey, thanks for going with me."

"No problem." I could smell her shampoo. Paul Mitchell, the kind that smelled like coconut.

Nikki's cousin Vanessa did want to go to the mall, which meant that all four of us—me, Beth, Nikki, and Vanessa—were crammed into the front seat of my Nissan pickup. It was an '86, it had over two hundred thousand miles on it, and the first thing Vanessa said when she climbed in was, "Is this your uncle's truck? Nikki said you live with your uncle and that he's really old and weird. Is this what he drives?"

"Nope, it's mine," I said. "I bought it myself."

"My uncle is not weird," Beth said, kicking Nikki's foot. "And he's not *that* old. He's forty-two."

"Is that how old this truck is?" asked Vanessa. She scanned the dashboard. "Where's the CD player? Where's the radio?"

I backed out of Nikki's driveway. "Nikki and Vanessa, you two need to share the side seat belt. And Beth, you need to put on the one in the middle. You know that."

Vanessa whispered something in Nikki's ear about the truck smelling like pepperoni, and the two of them cracked up. Beth eyed me reproachfully as she buckled up.

"My friend in Raleigh?" Vanessa said. "Her big sister drives a red Miata. It's adorable. That's what I'm going to get when I turn sixteen."

"Me, too," Nikki chimed.

"Not me," Beth said. "I'm going to get a BMW convertible."

I lifted my eyebrows. In Buckhead, the part of Atlanta we lived in, practically everyone drove expensive cars: Mercedes, BMWs, Saabs. That was one reason I loved my beat-up old pickup, even if it did smell like pepperoni. And actually, it wasn't pepperoni. It was sausage. On Saturday nights I worked for Entrées on Trays, a catering service that did deliveries for a handful of different restaurants, and last week I'd picked up five orders of cannelloni from The Mad Italian. The smell did kind of linger, but I didn't care. I thought Beth didn't either.

"Hey, Vanessa," I said, "Beth says you just moved here from North Carolina. What do you think of Atlanta so far?" I wouldn't have asked, except I thought I should give her another chance. After all, she was just a kid.

"Tacky," she said. "It's like the tackiest place ever—that's what my mom says. When we were driving here from Raleigh, we passed a huge water tower shaped like a butt."

Nikki and Beth giggled.

"It's not a butt," I said. "It's a giant peach. Anyway, the water tower you're talking about is in South Carolina, not Georgia."

"Whatever. It looked like a humongous butt."

I shut up for the rest of the ride. Vanessa entertained Nikki and Beth by describing, in detail, a book she'd gotten for her birthday called *How to Upscale Your Image*. "There's an entire chapter just about lipstick," she said at one point. "Like how it's really important to keep your lips moisturized, so you can apply your lipstick in an even coat. Of course, I don't have to wear lipstick if I don't want to, because I already have natural lip color. Not many people do."

I must have groaned, because Beth glared at me before turning to Vanessa and asking, "What about me? Do I have natural lip color?"

Vanessa squinted. "Maybe if you chewed on them a little."

"Beth, you do not need to chew on your lips," I said. "They're fine." I wanted to tell them that none of them needed to wear makeup, period. They were in the fifth grade, for christsake. But they'd moved from lipstick to eye shadow, and Beth nodded as Vanessa explained how to make close-set eyes appear farther apart by applying dark shadow to the outer corner of each lid.

Then I started thinking, hell, maybe I should be the one paying attention. With Kate, I never worried about how I looked. It wasn't important, and besides, she was beautiful enough for both of us. People treated me differently when I was with her, as if some of her spark rubbed off on me. Cuteness by association.

"And if your skin tone is uneven—see how Lissa's face is all blotchy?—well, that's when you'd use base. No offense, Lissa."

I dropped off Beth and her friends at the mall and told them to meet me at Chick-fil-A at two o'clock. I parked my truck and walked across the street to Cost Cutters, where I had an 11:00 appointment. I'd planned on simply getting a back-to-school trim, but now, after listening to Vanessa for the entire car ride, I found myself considering something more drastic. Maybe short hair would look good on me. Something soft around my face, maybe some layers . . .

Wait. I was letting a ten-year-old influence how I cut my hair? I'd worn my hair the same way for the last three years—

shoulder length, the ends slightly turned under—and except for a disastrous attempt to grow out my bangs, I'd liked it just fine.

I wondered what Kate would say if I cut it short. Kate had great hair: blond and thick and really soft, not coarse like mine. She used to get me to play with it when I spent the night at her house. She'd put her head in my lap while we watched TV, then close her eyes while I ran my fingers over her scalp.

Last summer we put lemon juice on our hair to add highlights, and afterward, when she stood in the sun, the strands around Kate's face glowed like gold. My hair turned kind of orange-y.

"Auburn," Kate said.

"Yeah, right," I responded.

Now my hair was back to its usual dull brown, and the more I thought about it, the more I decided that a short haircut was just the thing to get me out of this rut. What kind of wimp was I if I couldn't take a risk?

"I need a change," I told the stylist, whose name was Marcia. "Something kind of feathered around my face? Well, no, not feathered, exactly, but—"

"Something classy," Marcia said. She ran her fingers through my hair, lifting it in her hands as if weighing it. "A wedge. An asymmetrical wedge."

I should have known right then that I was making a mistake. I should have gotten up and run. "No, um, that's not really what I—"

"Oh, honey, it'll be *perfect*." She leaned closer and pressed her hands against my cheeks. "You have an oval-shaped face.

See? You need something perky and full to bring out your eyes. Do you ever wear eyeliner?"

"Well, no, not usually. Eyeliner kind of scares me. I don't like touching my eyeballs, and I don't think—"

"You should consider wearing eyeliner, hon. You have lovely eyes." She patted my shoulders and straightened up. "All right. Let's get this show on the road!"

I didn't end up with an asymmetrical wedge, thank God, but it couldn't have been much worse if I had. I finally convinced Marcia that I didn't want to go super, super short, and so she chopped off my hair at this awful mid-cheek length that made me look like an Eastern European refugee. It was just short enough that I couldn't tuck it behind my ears without it falling in my face, and just long enough that it wouldn't stay in place if I raked it back with my fingers. In fact, if I'd gotten a super-short haircut and had been trying to grow it out for a couple of months, this is how it would look. I had gotten my hair cut in an awkward, growing-out stage. I had *paid* to get my hair cut in an awkward, growing-out stage. I even left Marcia a tip.

"What did you do to your *hair*?" Vanessa said when I arrived at Chick-fil-A.

"I cut it," I said. I resisted the urge to try to push it behind my ears.

"Well, duh," Vanessa said. "But *why*? Are you going to go to school like that?"

Beth looked mortified. She busied herself gathering their empty cups and refused to meet my eyes.

On the drive home, while Beth, Nikki, and Vanessa tried out each other's new lip balms, I mentally rehearsed my rules for future living. Never make a major hair change without thinking about it for at least a day. Never make a major hair change at Cost Cutters. And regardless of how horrible life is, don't think a new look will solve the problem.

CHAPTER 3

I DROVE AROUND FOR A WHILE after dropping off Beth and her friends. I wasn't due at work for a couple more hours, but I didn't feel like hanging out at home. I turned right, and then left, and then left again, and before I knew it I was parked down the street from Kate's house, staring at her window from the front seat. I knew she wasn't there—her Jeep wasn't in the driveway—but I didn't care. I'd been thinking about her all day; at least this way I had something to focus on.

What I'd been turning over in my head was the fact that just because the two of us kissed, it didn't have to *mean* anything. Friends did that kind of stuff sometimes. Not to the extent that we did, maybe, but girls at school walked around with their arms slung over each other's shoulders, and I'd seen guys on the football team slap each other on the butt more times than I wanted to count. Plus, Kate was a very physical person to begin with—that's just the way she was.

She used to clutch my arm in the theater when we watched scary movies, and if my shirt tag was ever sticking out or my collar was messed up, she'd reach over and fix it without giving it a second thought.

It actually took me a while to get used to how touch-y she was, back when we first started hanging out. Jerry wasn't much of a hugger, even when he first moved in, and by the time I was in junior high, he'd pretty much stopped touching me altogether. So the first time Kate hugged me—it was after she got an A– on a science test that I'd helped her study for— I stiffened without meaning to.

"What?" Kate said, pulling away. "You act like I'm your Great-Aunt Lucy or something."

"I don't have a Great-Aunt Lucy," I said.

"You know what I mean. Do I have peanut-butter breath? Is that it?" She cupped her hand around her mouth and exhaled.

"No, it's just . . ." I shrugged. "I guess it's been a long time since someone's touched me." I realized how weird that sounded, and I blushed.

"Oh. Does it bother you? I mean, should I not hug you?"

"No, it's okay."

"Good," Kate said. "Touching is good."

I wondered if she remembered saying that. I wondered, if I brought it up, if she'd deny it. But that's what I wanted to tell her, that one person touching another person was perfectly normal. It's just that we'd been drinking that night at Rob's—she'd been drinking, anyway—and so things went further than they should have.

I thought of her hand on my skin, under my shirt. The

surprise of it, my sharp intake of breath. My pulse quickened now in the truck, and I shoved the memory away. For several minutes I held myself still—eyes closed, head back against the seat. Then a car drove by, and I jerked to attention.

A blue Saturn. Not Kate.

Of course not Kate. She was probably at the movies, because she always went to the movies on Saturday afternoons. We used to go together, and sometimes after one show, we'd sneak past the usher into another. Only today she'd be with Ben. She'd have her popcorn and her pink and blue heart candies from the Candy Jar, which she ate together to mix salty with sweet, and Ben would have his arm around her shoulder. Or maybe he'd rub her neck like he did that night at Rob's party, after they found us at the gazebo. Slow, lazy circles, while Kate relaxed and leaned closer.

I twisted the key in the ignition. It was stupid, lurking outside Kate's house like this. I never should have come.

At the Old Corner Bookstore, the clerks pretty much let you fend for yourself, which I liked. I knew I didn't want to go home and truly be alone—which was different, somehow, than being alone in a crowded store—and so I'd driven here with the vague notion of finding some way to get Kate out of my head. I stood inside the front entrance for a moment, then frowned and headed for the section labeled "Self-help." I didn't know what I was looking for, but I figured that was as good a place to start as any.

The first book I picked up was a book on candles called *Light Your Inner Fire*. I riffled through the first couple of chapters, then flipped to the back and found a chart indicating what color candle you should burn to achieve spiritual harmony. It had to do with when you were born. If you were born in January, your candle color was midnight blue, and if you were born in April, like Kate, your candle color was dusty rose. I was born in October, and according to the chart, my birth candle was brown. Not black, a Halloween-y color that at least had drama, but brown. I didn't know candles even came in brown.

I reshelved the candle book and moved farther down the aisle. Aroma therapy, past-life regression, astral projection . . .

Hmm. I'd heard of astral projection; it had to do with letting your spirit leave your body and go floating around the universe. As a concept, it had potential—talk about a great way to escape your problems. But the book I pulled out bugged me. On the cover a dreamy-looking woman lay face up in a field, while her astral self rose gently from her body. That part I could handle. What bothered me was the fact that her astral self was naked, but her physical self was wearing a peach leotard. It made no sense.

I glanced around, suddenly embarrassed to be here. The only other woman in this section wore a flowing shirt and a crystal necklace, and yes, that was definitely patchouli I smelled. I put back the book on astral projection and was heading for the exit when the title of a light blue paperback caught my eye. It was called *Lucid Dreaming: The Power of Being Awake and Aware in Your Dreams*. I tugged it free. The notes on the back said the author was a professor at Stanford, that he worked in something called a "sleep research center."

I paused. Placing too much importance on dreams was

awfully New Age–y, but the author of this book had a Ph.D. The cover photo showed him wearing a white lab coat and glasses. I turned to the first chapter and scanned the page.

"Being 'awake in your dreams' provides the opportunity for unique and compelling adventures rarely surpassed elsewhere in life," I read. "Yet adventure may prove to be the least important of a variety of reasons to cultivate the skill of lucid dreaming. For example, lucid dreaming has considerable potential for promoting personal growth and self-development, enhancing self-confidence, improving mental and physical health, facilitating creative problem-solving, and helping you to progress on the path to self-mastery."

I weighed the book in my hand, then thought, *What the hell*, and strode to the cash register. I felt silly as the guy behind the counter read the title, but I hugged my arms across my chest and tried to act nonchalant.

"Here you go," he said, passing me the book with the receipt stuck inside. He tapped his fingers against the counter. "Dreams, huh? Does it tell you how to interpret them? Because I had one a couple of nights ago that was absolutely wild."

He wanted me to ask about it, I could tell, but I smiled noncommittally and headed for the door.

CHAPTER

4

DARLIN DUPRIEST, THE WOMAN WHO RAN Entrées on Trays, met me at the door when I showed up at 5:15. I'd come straight from the bookstore, and I was a little early.

"My dear," she said, placing her hand on her chest. "Don't you look fabulous."

I blushed. Darlin was always fussing over me, complimenting my outfit or brushing lint off my shirt. Usually I liked it, even if I acted like I didn't, but this time my embarrassment was real. I looked nowhere near fabulous, not with my shorn hair.

"I have wonderful news," she said, pulling me inside. "I've finally hired a second driver, and she is *such* a doll."

"That's great," I said. For about a month now I'd been doing all the Saturday night deliveries myself, ever since Harold Schwartz fell in love with a girl named Tina and decided to work only on Fridays. I'd miss the extra tips, but

Saturday was the busiest night of the weekend, which was why I'd been hired in the first place. Having a second driver again would definitely make things more manageable.

"I have snacks in the parlor," Darlin said. "We can sit and chat until she arrives."

In the parlor, which to anyone else would be the living room, Darlin watched as I tried one of her small golden tarts. For Darlin, every snack, side dish, and main course deserved the utmost care, which I guess was why she started Entrées on Trays. Even though she was delivering restaurant orders instead of her own creations, she was still working with food.

"Mmm," I said, reaching for another. "What are they?"

"Spicy mushroom wheels," Darlin said. "Burl about fainted, he liked them that much. Made with Blue Plate mayonnaise, of course, since he won't eat any other."

Burl was Darlin's boyfriend. He and Darlin liked to watch *Antiques Roadshow* together, and whenever he came over, Darlin would fix elaborate trays of appetizers for them to munch on. I'd met Burl only once. He was a narrow, stoop-shouldered man with circles beneath his eyes, and when he'd glanced at me from the sofa, I'd thought of a mole. He'd mumbled an unintelligible greeting, then gone back to his bean dip.

"Did you know you can't get Blue Plate mayonnaise anywhere but the South?" Darlin asked.

"Huh," I said. I tried to think how to respond. "Has that been a problem for Burl? I mean, when he goes out of town?"

Darlin looked surprised, as if she'd never considered that before. "You know, I'm not sure he's ever been out of town. Now isn't that something?" The phone rang, and she rose from the sofa. "Give me a minute, hon. Bet you anything it's Pete Rossey wanting his scampi from the Crab Shack."

She crossed the room and picked up the phone. "Entrées on Trays," she said. She winked at me. "You bet, Mr. Rossey. How about some leafy greens to go with it? Got to keep those tubes clear, after all."

I took one more mushroom wheel, listening to Darlin and marveling at how easy and natural she acted with someone she'd never met face to face. That was probably my favorite thing about Darlin, how comfortable she seemed with herself. I wished I were more like that.

Kate met Darlin once, and I could tell she didn't like her. She didn't come right out and say it, but I saw her eyes travel from Darlin's wide hips to the collar of her blouse, where a roll of white skin pushed up from her bra strap. I saw how Kate hugged her arms around her ribs, as if reassuring herself that she would never be fat like that. And later, when Kate and I were alone, I made things worse by describing the Slim-Fast six-pack I'd seen in the back of Darlin's pantry, so old it was coated with dust.

"Oh, ick," Kate had said, laughing and covering her face. "Seriously, that is just so pitiful. I feel sorry for her. Don't you?"

I looked at Darlin now and felt ashamed.

She hung up the phone. "Well," she said, "I suppose you better head on over to the Crab Shack." She glanced at her watch. "I really wanted you to meet Ariel, though. I thought she'd be here by now."

I shrugged. I'd worked with Harold Schwartz for three months before he decided to cut back his hours, and the most we'd ever talked was when he needed directions from Alpharetta to Mary Mac's Tea Room. I liked it that way.

I slipped into my white caterer's jacket and grabbed my cash bag and walkie-talkie. "Want me to bring you anything?"

"Maybe a Reuben," Darlin said. "Or if someone orders from Fat Matt's, maybe some ribs?"

"Right," I said. "See you later."

A little before 7:00, as I was on my way to Babette's Café for an order of cassoulet, I heard a voice that wasn't Darlin's over the walkie-talkie.

"Uh, Ariel here," she said. There was the dead-air sound that meant she'd let go of the talk button, and then a click that meant she'd pressed it down again. "Over," she added.

I smiled. I'd had trouble with the walkie-talkies when I first started, too. And I still felt goofy saying, "Over" and "Ten-four."

"Good girl," said Darlin, her voice rich and full, despite the tinny reception. "I've got a pick-up for you at Canoe, going to 112 Arbor Gate Drive. Over."

"I'm on my way," Ariel said. "Over."

"Got one for you, too, Lissa. Stop by Sotto Sotto before delivering your Babette's order. It'll save you the trip back. Over."

I picked up the walkie-talkie and pressed the talk button. "Ten-four," I said. "Over."

She gave me the second address, along with the nearest big intersection for reference, and I did a quick calculation of the best route to get there. Then I picked up both orders and headed north on Peachtree Road. Taillights danced in front of me, and the smell of warm bread drifted from the carrying case to my right. This was what I loved about this job, the smooth peace of being alone on the road. It reminded me of being little, of driving somewhere late at night and hearing Mom and Dad chat softly in the front seat. Sometimes Dad talked about stars, which he'd loved. I remembered him telling Mom how the stars were all moving away from each other, and Mom saying something about how sad that was. But Dad said no, that was just the way the universe worked. Everything changed. It was a fact of life.

Mainly what I remembered was how safe I felt, with Beth asleep in her car seat and my head resting against the window. Mom would rub Dad's neck when he got tired, and he'd reach over and rest his hand on her thigh.

"Uh, Darlin?" Ariel said over the walkie-talkie. "I think I'm lost." Dead air, and then a click. "Over."

I frowned. I waited a few seconds, not wanting to give up the floaty feeling I'd achieved. But it was too late. I raised my walkie-talkie and pressed the talk button.

"Um, hi," I said. "This is Lissa. Darlin's probably not listening; she only uses the walkie-talkies to relay orders. Where are you? Over."

"Oh," Ariel said. "Well, I'm kind of near the big chicken. Under it, actually." She laughed nervously. "There are all these cars behind me. I think I'm causing a traffic jam."

I started to reply, but she cut back in.

"Over," she said. And then, "Sorry. I keep forgetting."

A heaviness settled inside me. First of all, the big chicken, which was literally this huge fake chicken guarding a KFC off

Highway 41, was way out by Marietta—nowhere near Ariel's destination. But on top of that, there was something about Ariel's voice that niggled at my brain. It sounded familiar, although I knew I didn't know anyone named Ariel.

I raised my walkie-talkie. "Take 41 south to West Paces Ferry—that'll take you about fifteen minutes. From there it's not that hard." I gave her directions, which she repeated. "Well, good luck," I said. "Over."

"Thanks," she said. "Over."

I put the walkie-talkie on the seat and tried to ease back into autopilot. I turned right off Peachtree onto East Wesley, appreciating the diminished traffic. I relaxed my shoulders, which I hadn't even realized were tense.

"Hey," Ariel said, cutting back into the silence. "These walkie-talkies are pretty cool, aren't they? I mean, we could be spies. Or security guards. Or *truckers*, yeah. What's your twenty, good buddy? Want to form a convoy?"

My fingers gripped the steering wheel.

"Lissa? You still there? Oh, hey—there's East Conway." I heard car horns and the squeal of brakes, and then an abrupt silence, which meant that Ariel had released the talk button. I grimaced, imagining why.

"So anyway," Ariel said, coming back on and sounding as if nothing out of the ordinary had happened. "What were you saying?"

I grabbed my walkie-talkie. I took a deep breath and tried to sound reasonable "Listen, we should really leave the line open in case Darlin needs to get through. Over."

"Ten-four," Ariel said. "Guess I'll keep on trucking, then. Watch out for the smokeys, you hear?"

I jammed down the button. I couldn't help myself. "CBs. Not walkie-talkies. Truckers use CBs, okay?"

"Hokey-dokey," Ariel said. "But they're pretty much the same thing, aren't they? Oops—missed my turn. Over and out, good buddy!"

I pulled into the driveway of the Babette's lady, coming to a hard stop. I was annoyed with myself for getting so irritated with Ariel, and I was annoyed with Ariel for being irritating. And I'd finally figured out who she reminded me of: Kimberly Thomas, a girl in my grade who had the same habit of going on and on about irrelevant topics. Kimberly believed in UFOs, for example, and she had a bumper sticker on her Volvo that said, "Ship Happens." Her research paper in last year's English class was on alien abductions, which she claimed to have experienced. "See this nose ring?" I once heard her say. "Believe me, it's not what you think."

Ariel and Kimberly had the same lilting speech pattern, the same flower-child way of saying whatever came to their minds. And the same way of sounding so incessantly cheerful that I wanted to scream.

I turned off the truck and let my head fall back against the headrest. Just because my life sucked didn't mean everyone else's did, and Ariel could be cheerful if she wanted to. More power to her. Just, God, let her be cheerful with someone else.

I took the Babette's order up to the house. The lady who answered the door pursed her lips.

"I've been waiting and waiting," she complained, taking the white paper bag I pulled from the carrier.

"Just be glad you don't live on Arbor Gate," I said under my breath.

"Excuse me?"

"Nothing. I'm sorry."

She sniffed and handed me a twenty-dollar bill, which, after subtracting $18.58 for her order, left me a whopping tip of $1.42.

I put the money in my bag and turned to go.

"Young lady?" the woman said. "My change?"

I looked back, saw that she was serious, and grimly counted out her change. Back in the truck, I shifted into reverse and pulled onto East Wesley. I'd gone only half a mile when Ariel's voice blared from the walkie-talkie.

"Breaker, breaker, good buddy. This is Red Rover to Blue Bandit. Over."

I snatched the walkie-talkie. I pressed the talk button. "What?"

"Uh, should I be seeing signs for Stone Mountain? I think maybe I—"

Static drowned her out. I only caught a couple more words—something about a shortcut, something about I-85—before her signal disappeared completely.

I wanted to enjoy it. I wanted to put everything out of my mind and to sink into the solitude of the dark Atlanta night. But if Ariel had any sense at all, she'd pull off the highway and turn around. It wouldn't be long before she'd be back in range.

At 9:30, I pulled into Darlin's driveway and cut the motor. Parked in front of me was a pale blue Volvo, and on the bumper was a white bumper sticker. "Ship Happens," it said in black letters.

No, I thought. *It can't be.* But Ariel's voice still rang in my head. She'd gotten lost three more times during the course of the night, and the more I replayed her chirpy "Um, Lissa?"s, the more I realized that yes, it could be and almost definitely was. How else could I explain the identical blue Volvo?

Unless there were hundreds of Kimberly/Ariel clones wheeling across the city in their spaceship-mobiles. My head throbbed in protest. I grabbed my stuff and climbed out of the truck, squaring my shoulders and heading to the house.

"Come in, come in," Darlin said when she opened the door. "I hear you've had quite a night!"

A few feet behind her stood Kimberly Thomas. Her face lit up and she said, "Lissa! As in *Lissa* Lissa, from sophomore English. I thought it was you!"

I thought it was you, too, I wanted to say. *And I wish it weren't.* Instead, I glanced at Kimberly's burgundy hair and heavy eyeliner and said, "I don't get it. Why'd you tell Darlin your name was Ariel?"

"Because my name is Ariel," she said.

"Your name is Kimberly," I said.

She waved her fingers in the air. "On my birth certificate, sure. But my spiritual name is Ariel."

I handed my walkie-talkie and my cash bag to Darlin, raising my eyebrows like *are you getting this?*

Darlin smiled and placed my things on the hall table. She picked up a Styrofoam container of what looked like Uno's cheese sticks and dipped one in marinara. "My real name is Deirdre," she said. "*Such* a bad fit. I changed it to Darlin when I was twenty-nine."

"'Darlin' is a thousand times better than 'Deirdre,'" Kimberly/Ariel said. "So much softer."

35

I stared at them both.

"Cheese stick?" Darlin said, holding out the box.

"No, thanks."

"I'll take one more," Kimberly/Ariel said.

I watched her scoop up a blob of marinara, and I thought, *Wait a minute, I didn't bring those to Darlin.* And Darlin didn't ask Kimberly to bring them, either, because I'd have overheard it if she had. Which meant that Kimberly thought to bring them on her own.

I folded my arms over my chest. Good ol' Kimberly had brought Darlin cheese sticks, while in all the chaos I'd forgotten Darlin's Reuben completely. Although why should it matter? It wasn't like I owned Darlin. Other people could do nice things for her, too. Still, my mood plunged from bad to worse.

"Well, good night," I said, wanting suddenly to be gone. I slipped out of my caterer's jacket and headed for the door.

"Yeah, I've got to go, too," Kimberly said. "Hold on, Lissa. I'll walk out with you. Bye, Darlin! See you next weekend!"

Outside, she jogged to catch up with me.

"Thanks for helping me tonight," she said as I climbed into my truck. "I thought I knew Atlanta pretty well, but obviously I don't."

I gave her a tight smile. She was blocking me from shutting the door.

"Seriously, there are so many streets that I've never even heard of. Argonne Drive, Tuxedo, Slaton . . ." She rose up on her toes, peering into the truck. "Hey, what are you reading?" she asked, spotting my dream book on the dashboard.

I grabbed the book and hid it in my lap, but part of the

title must still have been visible. Her eyes dipped down and she said, "Dreams. Cool. I didn't know you were into that stuff."

My face grew hot. "I'm not." The receipt was still sticking out, and I tugged it free and crumpled it in my palm. "I just . . . I happened to run across it and . . . I'm *not*."

"Okay," Kimberly said. "Whatever." She hesitated, then tilted her head. "Listen, it's not even ten o'clock. You want to do something? Go get some Krispy Kremes?"

I wanted to get Krispy Kremes with Kimberly about as much as I wanted to return to Cost Cutters for an entire beauty makeover. I put the key in the ignition and started the truck. "Sorry," I said. "I'm beat."

"Yeah, okay," she said. She stepped away from the truck, and for a second I felt bad, especially when I saw that she was blushing.

But it wasn't my problem. I shifted into reverse and backed out of the drive.

C H A P T E R

5

ALL DAY SUNDAY I STAYED IN THE HOUSE. I did my homework, mainly, and helped Beth with hers. Then, after dinner, I tried to read the first chapter of my dream book. It was interesting, but I'd lost my earlier enthusiasm. It bugged me that Kimberly had seen my book. That she, of all people, thought it was "cool."

But that's dumb, I told myself. It was like saying, "Ew, she touched my cupcake, so I don't want it anymore." Still, I closed the book.

On Monday, I woke up late and had to rush to get dressed. I'd hoped my hair would somehow look normal again, but if anything, it looked worse. In some places it lay matted to my head, while in other places it did this awful winged-back thing, and nothing I did could make it hang straight. I briefly considered wearing a hat—that's how desperate I was—but the only hat I owned was a green felt fedora I'd worn to a costume party in the eighth grade. I'd gone as Robin Hood to Kate's Maid Marian.

"Try some mousse," Beth said. She stood half inside my room, leaning against the door frame.

"Beth, I don't do mousse," I told her. "And besides, I don't have any."

"I do."

I put down my brush and turned around. "You do? Since when?"

"Want me to get it?"

She showed me how much to smear into my hair, and with her help I managed to fluff out the sections that were clumped to my head. It still looked terrible, though. Beth and I agreed.

At school, I kept my eyes on the floor and hurried to my homeroom. I kept expecting people to comment on my hair, but no one said a word. "Hey, Lissa," said a girl named Terri, "got the math assignment?" But that was it. The only person who noticed was Ms. Horowitz, who was my homeroom teacher and also my science teacher. "Nice haircut," she said as she moved down the aisle distributing handouts. Terri lifted her head and studied me more closely. "Oh yeah," she said. Then she went back to her math.

Fourth period was American history, which Kate and I had together. I quickly scanned the room, hating myself for feeling nervous, then walked to the back row and sat down. A guy named Scott thunked into the seat beside me and dropped his backpack. "Mitch, buddy," he said, punching his friend on the shoulder. "What'd you think of Jodi's party, huh?"

I pulled out my textbook and flipped it open. My head felt

lighter without long hair, and I could sense the section to the left of my part starting to flip out again. I smoothed it down, keeping my eyes on my book and maintaining what I hoped was a neutral expression.

Kate was the last to arrive. She hesitated, then took the empty desk next to Missy Colquitt. *Oh, Kate,* I thought, *Missy Colquitt? Instead of me?* Missy wore stretch pants and big hoop earrings, and she phrased everything in extremes, as in, "Omigod, could I be more excited than I am at this moment? Seriously, could I be more excited?"

But maybe Kate liked Missy these days. Maybe they were best buds. It wasn't as if Kate hadn't changed in other ways. Like how she dressed, for example. Today she wore a light blue T-shirt and jeans. Girls' jeans, cut to "show off her curves," as her mom would say.

Kate used to hate girls' jeans. We liked them faded and loose, beat-up old Levis that had already been broken in.

Mr. Neilson droned for twenty minutes about western expansion, then told us to get into groups and make time lines. Kate looked at Missy, and the two of them scooted their desks together. "Just don't expect me to be any help," I heard Missy complain. "I mean, could I be less motivated?"

"Lissa?" Mr. Neilson said. "Do you have a group?"

I glanced around. "Uh . . ."

"Why don't you work with Scott and Mitch. Guys, make room for Lissa."

"Sure," Scott said. "We're stuck on the gold rush. Do you know when the second wave started?"

We'd been working for about fifteen minutes when I felt someone standing above me. I raised my head.

"You cut your hair," Kate said. She was wearing eyeliner and mascara, which I hadn't noticed until now. Another change.

"Yep," I said.

"It looks good."

"Yeah, right. You don't have to lie, Kate."

"Lissa, I wasn't—" She shook her head. "I'm just surprised. I thought you liked it long."

"Well, now it's short."

"I know."

I concentrated on my breathing. With her so close, all I could think about was how it felt when her skin touched mine. I didn't want to, but I couldn't help it. It made my legs feel heavy.

"I just wanted to say I liked it, okay?" She glanced at Mitch and Scott and shut her mouth. "Never mind. This is ridiculous." She turned around and strode across the room.

Mitch waited until she was out of earshot, then whistled. "Damn, that girl is hot." He glanced in my direction. "She your friend?"

"Shut up, man," Scott said. "She's taken. Now come on, we've only got a couple of minutes to get this done."

"Who's she dating?" Mitch said.

"Ben Porter. You want to take him on?"

Mitch grinned and tapped his pen against his leg. "Nah, not today. But *damn* is she hot."

I hunched over my notebook and tried to make my heart quit pounding. It wasn't Kate's angry tone, or the fact that she stormed away—it was the way my chest tightened just being near her.

Calm down, I told myself. *Breathe.* I mean, fine, I felt something for another girl. Felt it stronger than maybe I'd admitted. Except it wasn't just "another girl" I was talking about; it was Kate. And when friends were as close as we were, well, maybe that closeness took on a lot of different forms, and maybe that meant things got confused sometimes. Like when a little kid said he wanted to grow up and marry his mom— that didn't mean that's what he really wanted.

Shit. What if *she* wanted to work things out between us, and I'd blown it by being such a jerk?

Last spring, sitting outside the cafeteria, someone asked a bunch of us which we'd rather be if we had to choose: smart or nice. Missy said, "Nice," along with most of the people in the group. Kate and I said, "Smart," and we grinned at each other, knowing each other's minds. "Because if all you are is nice," Kate explained to me later, "then you can't choose to be smart. But if you're smart, you can choose to be nice."

"Exactly," I said.

But now it seemed I was neither. Could I be more pathetic? I glanced at Kate's back, at the way her hair spilled over her shirt, and dropped my eyes.

Ben found me during lunch. He straddled the chair beside me and grinned like we were old friends. "Lissa. What's up?"

I eyed him, then went back to my macaroni and cheese. Around us, kids chatted and laughed, and the cafeteria had that overcrowded feeling of too many bodies crammed into one place. The air smelled like steamed vegetables.

"Haven't seen you in a while," Ben said. "You go to Jodi's on Saturday?"

I didn't respond.

"Lissa, listen," he said. "This thing between you and Kate—you've got to work it out. She's really torn up about it."

"Uh-huh, and that's why she hasn't talked to me for two weeks straight." I neglected to mention our encounter in history. That wasn't really talking.

"She says you're the one who won't talk to her."

I put down my fork. "I don't want to do this, Ben."

"It was that night at Rob's house, wasn't it? The weekend before school started. Did you have a fight or something?"

My stomach clenched. There was no way Kate had told him, I knew that, but even coming this close to the truth made me feel dizzy. "Yeah," I said. "We had a fight. It was stupid. It was over this sweatshirt she borrowed." I checked his expression.

"A *sweatshirt*? You two aren't speaking to each other over a sweatshirt?"

I wadded up my napkin. I shoved it under the edge of my plate and slid my glass over to trap it in place. "So . . . did Kate's mom ever find out about her tattoo?"

Ben rubbed the bridge of his nose. "Yeah, she saw it when Kate was getting ready for school one morning."

"Was she mad?"

"Are you kidding? She wanted Kate to go back and get it removed."

"Did she?"

"You can't remove a tattoo, Lissa. Once it's done, it's done."

I frowned. You *can* remove a tattoo; it's just difficult. And supposedly it's pretty painful. Some things, on the other hand, can't be undone.

I looked at Ben, but I had nothing to say.

CHAPTER

6

AFTER SUPPER, I HOLED UP IN MY ROOM and got my dream book back out. I read for an hour or so, then leaned back against my pillow, thinking about what I'd learned. According to the book, the average person sleeps for a third of her life. And when you sleep, you dream—at least part of the time, anyway. Which means that the smart thing to do is to figure out how to learn from your dreams so that you're not wasting all those hundreds of hours.

I wanted to believe that was true. I wanted to believe I could make a difference in my life, as long as I was willing to put in the work. And the way the author talked made it seem possible. I'd read through chapter six now, and I'd gotten past the technical stuff to a more nuts-and-bolts section on lucid dreams. I loved the idea of a "lucid dream," a dream in which you're actually aware that you're dreaming. Aware in the same way as you're aware of things in your waking life, where you're able to choose to lift your hand or jump up and down or whatever. But if you were dreaming—and *aware* that you were dreaming—you could choose to fly. Or travel to another country, or to another world altogether. Anything you liked.

You could also use lucid dreaming to explore your own "normal" dreams, a possibility that scared me at the same time as it drew me in. The author said a lot of people used lucid dreaming to deal with recurrent nightmares. To explain, he talked about a little girl from Denver who kept having dreams about being attacked by a shark.

"But you know there aren't any sharks in Colorado," he told her.

"Of course not," she said.

"Well, since you know there aren't really any sharks where you swim, if you ever see one there again, it would be because you were dreaming. And once you know you're dreaming, you can do whatever you like—you could even make friends with the dream shark, if you wanted to!"

A week later he talked to the girl again, and she said, "Do you know what I did? I rode on the back of the shark!"

I liked that story, corny as it was, because for about as long as I could remember, I'd been having my own recurrent nightmare. Or maybe *nightmare* was too strong a term, since it wasn't as if I woke up screaming or anything. But it *was* unsettling, especially since it was a dream that was based on something real. When I was five—not in my dream, but in real life—I went with Mom to Service Merchandise. The checkout line was really long, so I asked if I could wait outside. Mom said okay, but to stay right in front of the store where she could see me. The next thing Mom knew, I was walking hand in hand across the parking lot with a man she'd never seen before. Mom ran out the door and yelled, "Lissa! *Lissa!*" and the man dropped my hand and fled.

Mom had told me that story a hundred times, and every time, it gave me the shivers. That's probably why I liked hearing it so much. But then I'd started having dreams about it, dreams in which I was walking off to be kidnapped, or worse. In my dreams I *knew* I should turn back, but I couldn't.

I'd had that dream a lot when I was younger, then less and less the older I got. Until recently. When I was a kid, Mom would sit with me after these dreams, stroking my hair until I fell back asleep. But Mom was no longer here to soothe me. The whole thing was stupid, I knew. I was sixteen. There was no way anyone was going to kidnap me. Who would want to? But the dream wasn't really about being kidnapped, not anymore. Maybe it was about this Kate stuff, how I'd walked smack into a big mistake and now I had to be careful what I did next. I wasn't sure.

But to banish the dream, maybe I had to find out. So after brushing my teeth and washing my face, I crawled into bed with the goal of having a lucid dream. I shifted around, smushing the pillow down just the right amount, and then I slid my feet farther into the cool sheets. I lay there, ready to begin, but my brain wouldn't calm down. Now that I was committed to trying this, I was scared of what might happen.

I smoothed my quilt over my chest, my fingers finding its nubbly seams. On my bedside table, my Felix the Cat alarm clock ticked its muted tick. On the other side of the bed was the tall chest of drawers Jerry had found at a garage sale, its shadow stretching over the wall. Everything was familiar. Everything was safe.

When at last I felt ready, I closed my eyes and tried an exercise in which I tensed and relaxed my muscles, working my way up from my toes to my head. With each muscle group, I imagined a flow of energy traveling up my body, spreading through me in a wave.

The exercise was supposed to bring me closer to the dream state, but I must have done something wrong, because all that tensing made me feel weak, like I was going to faint. Plus, somehow during the course of the exercise, I forgot about my stomach altogether. I skipped from my hips and lower back straight up to my shoulders. What did that mean, I wondered?

I kept with it, though, imagining a flow of energy moving through my body, and after a while my arms and legs started to tingle. The book said that if you felt odd vibrations, you were supposed to try and intensify them, so that's what I did. I relaxed my muscles and kind of *pushed* on the vibrations, like how you'd push on something if you were trying hard to remember it. The tingling sped up until my whole body hummed, including my heart, which whammed against my ribs. *Oh, God,* I thought. *What if I accidentally kill myself?*

I tried to pull out of it, but it was hard. My arms and legs felt leaden, and it took all of my strength to slide my hand out from under the sheet. I felt like I was moving under water. Finally I wrenched free, and everything went ZAP back to normal. My heart was no longer racing, and I could move my body again. And then I wished I hadn't gotten so freaked out, because maybe I'd been on the verge of doing it, of slipping into a lucid dream. What if I'd ruined it?

Not that it would have made much difference, because a minute later Beth pushed open my door and padded into my room. The light from the hallway spilled onto the floor.

47

"Lissa?" she whispered. "Are you awake?"

"No," I said. I was irritated that she'd barged in, because even though she didn't technically wake me up, she could have.

"Can I sleep with you?" she asked.

"I guess. But you better not talk."

"I won't." She walked to the other side of my bed and climbed in. "I'll scratch your back if you'll scratch mine. You can even go first."

I snorted. She meant that I could scratch her back first and be done with it, which was supposedly the best strategy, since it left me free to drift off as my own back was being rubbed. But Beth almost always fell asleep before fulfilling her end of the bargain. Still, I knew I'd be lying awake either way.

"Roll over," I said.

She flipped onto her stomach, and I started scratching. I listened as her breathing slowed. She sighed, and I wondered why she had woken up, what unwanted dreams had troubled her.

I smoothed down her hair. "Sleep tight," I whispered.

CHAPTER 7

AT SCHOOL, KATE AND I DANCED AROUND each other
like two like-charged magnets: close enough to keep tabs on
each other, but with an invisible force preventing us from
fully connecting. In history, she laughed too loudly at Missy
Colquitt's jokes, knowing I was watching, and in the cafeteria she sat one or two tables away when she could have chosen a seat at the opposite end of the room. For my part, I tried
to strike a balance between not staring at her and yet not
looking away if my glance did happen to fall on her, and
the result was that I was hyperaware of every move I made,
as if I were trying to act cool at a party where I felt totally out
of place.

So when I got home on Friday afternoon, I was almost
giddy with relief. The week was over and I didn't have to see
Kate until Monday, and I felt like I could breathe again. And
eat. I dropped my backpack on the table and opened the
refrigerator.

Pickles. Yogurt. Cold spaghetti left over from last night. Eggs. Applesauce. Half a stick of butter. Milk.

I closed the door and leaned against it. I wanted something comforting, something rich and fattening and full of calories. Homemade doughnuts. Grits casserole. Fried bologna sandwiches. When I was little, Mom used to make fried bologna sandwiches for me. The slice of bologna would puff up in the middle like a turtle shell, and Mom would slit it with a knife to make it lie flat on the bread. Then she'd cut the sandwich into four smaller sandwiches and serve them to me with apple juice and Goldfish crackers. While I ate, she'd tell me stories about my day: Lissa Gets Her Toenails Cut, Lissa Makes Up Her Bed, Lissa Finds the House Key and Saves the Day. Never anything remarkable, but the way she told them, she made me feel like a star.

Once I asked Jerry for a fried bologna sandwich, back when he first moved in with us. He didn't butter the pan, and the bottom of the sandwich turned black. I ate it anyway, eyes on my plate while Jerry read the paper, until he saw my expression and dumped what was left in the trash.

Kate's mom stocked their freezer with Lean Cuisines, and except for the times when her dad did the shopping, the only cookies in their pantry were fat-free oatmeal raisin. Jerry was a horrible cook and he knew it, but at least he made the effort. One time he invented a pretty good recipe for peanut butter–coconut bars, and every so often he whipped together a batch of fudge that we could snack on for days. The first time he tried, he turned the stove up too high, and the fudge hardened around the wooden spoon like cement around a flagpole. Jerry let the pan cool, then gave knives to Beth and me and let us chip off as many flakes as we wanted. Beth didn't remember, but I did.

I checked the contents of the pantry, but there were no tins of brownies I'd forgotten I'd made, no secret loaves of banana bread. From the den, I heard the old cartoons Beth loved: Bugs Bunny's wise-guy laugh and spurts of lively music. I tapped my thumbnail against my teeth, then reached to the top shelf and grabbed the graham crackers, which I set on the counter along with a jar of peanut butter, a box of raisins, and a bag of jumbo marshmallows. I grabbed two plates from the cabinet and got to work.

"What *is* it?" Beth asked when I presented her with my creation.

"It's a snack. I made you a snack. Aren't you hungry?"

"Not really." She poked the marshmallow and wrinkled her nose.

"Beth, it's good. It's like peanut-butter-and-marshmallow cream, which you love." I sat down beside her and took a bite, but the marshmallow made the peanut butter sandwich too tall, and raisins rained to the floor as I struggled to bite down. I'd tried pressing the raisins into the marshmallow—I thought it would look cheerful—but the marshmallow was too doughy and it didn't quite work.

"Mmm," I said. A raisin zinged the coffee table.

"Don't we have any potato chips?" Beth asked.

"Just try it, Beth."

She picked up her snack and took a small bite from the corner. Her expression stayed suspicious, but she took another bite. "Vanessa got elected class leader," she said with her mouth full.

"Oh yeah?"

"She gets to pass out all the handouts, and if Ms. Hutchinson needs a note taken to the office, she gets to take it."

"Huh."

We watched as Bugs Bunny stole a row of carrots from a neighbor's garden, pulling them from the soil as if he were ripping the seam from a pair of pants.

"And Toby Norton asked her to go steady with him, but she said no." Beth plucked the raisins from her marshmallow. "She says his teeth look like vomit."

"Beth."

"Well, they do. They're yellow and kind of speckled-y. I don't think he brushes them enough."

I finished my last bite of graham cracker and wiped the crumbs off my mouth. "What about Nikki? Are you two still best friends?" I liked Nikki. Nikki rescued daddy longlegs and wanted to be a firefighter when she grew up.

Beth shrugged. "Nikki's kind of babyish, don't you think? She doesn't even wear a bra."

"Beth, *you* don't wear a bra." I paused. "Do you?" I felt her shoulder for a strap and my eyebrows shot up. "Beth, you're in fifth grade. You don't *need* a bra. You don't even—"

I stopped. Maybe I was wrong. Maybe the other girls in her class were all wearing bras, all except Nikki, and so of course Beth had to, too. I didn't wear one until seventh grade, but I knew that was pretty late. And even then I'd had no idea how to buy one, or how to ask Jerry to buy one for me, which I was not going to do, and I still remembered how traumatic it was to go to Rich's lingerie department and riffle through the rows and rows of light, silky undergarments.

I bought my one white cotton bra and wore it day after day, until Kate's mom somehow found out and bought me another. She left it on Kate's bed one night when I was staying over, explaining that she'd found a buy-two-get-one-free sale at Neiman Marcus. "And Kate certainly doesn't need three new bras. If it doesn't fit, we can exchange it. All right, sweetie?"

"Where'd you get it?" I asked Beth.

She was mad at me for touching her, and she wrapped her arms around her ribs. "It's one of yours. An old one."

There was no way a bra of mine would fit Beth's skinny frame, even an old one. Maybe that's why she was wearing a sweatshirt. God, what a nightmare, going through fifth grade wearing your big sister's droopy bra.

I switched off the TV with the remote. "Why don't we go to Rich's and get you some of your own. All right? Let me write a note to Jerry telling him we'll be late for dinner."

Beth plucked at her jeans. "I want to go to Macy's," she said. "That's where Vanessa got hers. And we don't need to leave a note for Jerry, because he won't be here anyway. He left a message on the machine."

"Working late?"

"He said he was going to finish up some stuff, and then he and Sophie were going to grab a hamburger at Bennigan's."

"He and *Sophie*? Did he, like, ask her out? Like, on a date?"

"Lissa, please. This is Jerry, remember?"

Exactly, and Jerry was not a grab-a-hamburger kind of guy. Occasionally he took me and Beth to dinner, but he rarely went out on his own and never with his co-workers. He said situations like that made him uncomfortable, and he blamed it on how he was brought up. He was raised along with my dad on my grandparents' farm in Tennessee, where, according to Jerry, bread-and-mayonnaise sandwiches were considered a delicacy, and catching greased hogs at the state fair was the closest thing to culture they experienced. My dad went to college and taught himself to act more sophisticated, but Jerry was still a work in progress.

I thought about how idiotic I'd acted around Kate these last couple of weeks, and it occurred to me that when it came to social skills, Jerry and I were a lot alike. Maybe it was genetic. I winced as I remembered the way I stopped and studied a "Say No to Drugs" poster when Kate passed me in the hall this afternoon, just so I wouldn't have to meet her eyes. I had to tell myself all over again that it was the weekend, that for two and a half days I didn't have to deal with anything I didn't want to.

I stood up from the couch. "Come on, Beth. Let's go."

At Macy's lingerie department, we were approached by a pinched-lipped saleswoman wearing a lime green suit. "Can I help you?" she asked.

Beth stepped a foot or two away. She fingered the strap of a black silk slip, then moved on to examine a cream colored camisole.

"I think we're okay," I said. I headed for the junior-miss section, and Beth ducked her head and followed.

"Oh, you're shopping for your little sister," the saleswoman exclaimed. She walked beside us, her panty hose swishing between her thighs. "Is this your first, dear? Your first brassiere?" She whipped out a tape measure. "Raise your arms, and let's figure out your size."

Beth shot me a look of desperation.

"You know what, uh"—I checked her name tag—"Edith? I think we'll look on our own first. If we need any help, we'll find you." I steered Beth to a rack of nightshirts. "This one's cute," I said, pulling out a red-and-white baseball jersey with the word *Bazooka* spelled across the front. "You probably need something new to sleep in. What do you think?"

Edith frowned. "Well. Call me if you need me." She waited another moment, then swished away to assist another customer.

"Do I really need to be measured?" Beth asked, as I draped the nightshirt over my arm and led Beth to the rows of bras.

"Nah. Just try on a few to see which fits best." I selected some 30-As in different styles and handed them to her. "Start with these. You might have to adjust the straps."

She disappeared into the dressing room, then reemerged several minutes later. "I *think* it fits," she said. She stood very straight with her stomach tucked in and shoulders back.

"Does it lie flat against your skin? Does it feel like it'll stay in place if you move around?"

She walked a few steps away from me, lifting and lowering her shoulders like a strange gawky bird. Then she froze, reaching into her shirt to fish for an escaped strap. "Do they come any smaller?"

The style she finally selected was Warner's "My First Bra" in size 28-AA. We bought two: one white, one peach. Beth wanted to wear one immediately, so we made a pit stop at the bathroom so she could change. Since we had to cut through the food court anyway, we decided to get Chick-fil-A's and waffle fries, and afterward ice cream at Baskin-Robbins. Mint chocolate chip for me, bubble gum for Beth. The whole trip home, she spit chunks of gum into her hand, so that by the time we arrived, she had a huge pink wad to put back in her mouth and chew. I tried not to watch.

That evening, I made a point of going to Beth's room to say good night. I'd taken her to buy her first bra, and I felt like I'd handled it pretty well. Still, it should have been Mom. I thought again about my first bra. It should have been Mom for both of us.

Beth was only two when Mom and Dad died, so she didn't miss them in the same way I did. She asked about them occasionally, questions about what they were like or whether they thought she was cute as a baby. If I didn't know the answers, I made them up. But mainly I tried to do what they would have done if they were still alive. It wasn't enough, but it was the best I could offer.

I sat on the edge of Beth's bed and listened as she told me about a quiz she'd taken in *Seventeen*. It was called "Are You a Fashion Victim?" According to the quiz, Beth was a "fashion fiend," which apparently was a good thing. I let her go on until her voice grew drowsy, and then I leaned over and gave her a quick hug. As I pulled back, my fingers grazed her shoulder blade.

"Beth?" I said.

"Hmm?"

"Are you wearing your bra?"

"Hmm."

"Beth, you don't wear a bra to sleep in. You only wear it during the day."

"Okay," she mumbled.

"Well, don't you want to take it off?"

No answer. She was asleep.

C H A P T E R

8

I WOKE UP THE NEXT MORNING determined not to think about Kate. Anyway, I had plenty of other things to think about, like my incredibly dirty truck, for example, which I'd promised myself I would wash today. Inside and out, just in case Vanessa was right and it did smell like pepperoni. I threw on jeans and a sweatshirt and jogged downstairs, where Jerry stood at the stove making blueberry pancakes. He whistled as he flipped them in the skillet, and he made a special one for Beth in the shape of a B. He asked if I wanted an L. I told him I didn't think so, but thanks.

"So what'd you two do last night?" he asked, once we were seated at the table.

"Nothing," Beth said.

"We went shopping," I said. "And then we watched a movie on TV—*Sabrina*."

Beth put down her juice. "It was boring. The remake's better."

"Audrey Hepburn," Jerry mused. "I've always been fasci-nated with her. If you look at her features one by one, you realize she's actually fairly ordinary looking. But somehow, when you take in the whole picture, she comes across as beautiful." He stabbed a bite of pancake. "Strange, huh?"

I'd say. I'd never heard Jerry say word one about how beautiful a woman was, movie star or not. I didn't think he noticed that kind of thing.

"What about you?" I said. "What'd you do?"

"Stayed late updating some orders, then went to Benni-gan's with Sophie." He paused. "It was fun."

"You sound surprised."

"Nah, it's not that. It's just . . ." He carved off another bite of pancake, which he chewed and swallowed before downing a sip of coffee. When he spoke again, his tone was all busi-ness. "Gotta go in this afternoon. Resoil some azaleas. Either of you want to come?"

"I'm going to Vanessa's," Beth said. "We're giving each other makeovers."

"I've got some stuff to do, too," I said. "And I've got to be at Darlin's by five-thirty."

"Oh yeah," he said. "Today's Saturday, isn't it?" He stood up and took his dishes to the sink, then circled back and rested his hands on the back of the chair. He cleared his throat. "Listen, there's a chance I might be late again. Beth, think you can stay at Vanessa's while Lissa does her deliveries?"

"Sure," Beth said. "She said I could stay for dinner."

"Great. And Lissa'll pick you up when she's done." He looked at me and wrinkled his brow. "Unless you were plan-ning to go out."

I forced a smile. "Nope."

"All right, well, you two have a good one." He grabbed his jacket and banged through the screen door.

"Maybe it *was* a date," Beth said as soon as we heard his car start.

"Maybe."

"Hey," she snickered. "If *Jerry* can get a date . . ."

"Thanks, Beth. I love you, too."

"Lissa, I was kidding. Geez, can't you take a joke?"

I focused on my pancakes, sopping up as much syrup as possible with one double-stacked bite. I crammed it into my mouth, as sweet as I could stand.

After breakfast, I backed my pickup into the middle of the driveway and hosed it down. I filled a bucket with soapy water, grabbed some old towels from the garage, and started scrubbing. The monotony of the work was soothing, and I gave myself over to the warmth of the sun on my back and the back-and-forth pull on my biceps.

This isn't so bad, I found myself thinking. I was alone, yeah, and my only immediate plans were with my ten-year-old sister, but it wasn't like I was miserable or anything. I knew plenty of people who couldn't bear to be on their own—people who turned on the TV just for the sound of conversation, for instance—but not me. I could handle solitude just fine.

I was rinsing the last of the suds off the windshield when a car horn snapped me out of my daze. I jerked up, shoving my hair out of my eyes, because I knew that horn. It was Kate's horn. How many times had I heard it when she came to pick me up?

But the Jeep across the street was red, not black. A kid holding a baseball bat dashed out of the Albertsons' front door, yelling, "Good game! See you tomorrow!"

I braced myself on the hood of the truck. My heart whammed in my chest, and sweat pricked my armpits. Which was crazy, because it *wasn't* Kate; it was just some kid being collected by his mom. So why was I reacting like this? Why was my *body* reacting like this?

I walked to the side of the house and turned off the hose. I lowered myself to the grass, resting my elbows on my knees and letting my head fall forward. The sun warmed my neck and hair, and slowly, my body came back to me. I leaned against the brick wall, lifting my head and staring into space.

It wasn't just that I thought it was Kate. It was that I wanted it to be Kate and at the same time was terrified of it being Kate, although I knew that was ridiculous. I mean, I knew Kate as well as I knew myself. At least, I used to.

But if I didn't know Kate, then maybe I didn't know myself—and it was that not-knowing that made my gut clench. Like losing your balance, that whoosh of almost falling, before pulling yourself back in line.

I stood up. I grabbed a rag. I wiped the sides, the hood, the back of my truck, focusing only on the job at hand.

CHAPTER 9

"LISSA," DARLIN SAID when I showed up at her house that night. She sounded tired. "How are you, sweetie? Come on in, I've got your things on the table."

I stepped into the entryway and searched her face. Her mascara was smudged, and the lines around her mouth seemed more pronounced. "Um, I'm fine," I said. "How about you?"

"The truth? Not so good." Her voice trembled. "Burl called it quits. Said he felt smothered."

"Oh no," I said. "I'm sorry."

Darlin waved her hand and tried to laugh. "Well, you win some, you lose some. I'm sure you don't want to hear about an old lady's troubles."

I shifted my weight. I was sorry about her and Burl, but it wasn't like I knew him that well. I was afraid anything I said would make things worse.

"So . . . has Mr. Rossey called?" I finally asked. "Shrimp scampi as usual?"

Darlin looked blank. Then she straightened up and said, "Yes, yes. Shrimp scampi and a house salad, blue cheese on the side. You surely do know your customers, Lissa."

I felt bad that she would even say that. She was the one who knew the customers, not me. But I wasn't good at articulating that stuff, so instead I said, "What, uh, about Kimberly? Is she working tonight?"

"Ariel, you mean?"

"Right, Ariel. Whatever."

"She should be here any minute. That's one thing I did right, at any rate, getting you some help after all this time."

I tried to look appreciative.

"Oh, Lissa, I'm glad you and I stumbled across each other," Darlin said. She helped me into my caterer's jacket, smoothing my collar and patting my shoulders. "It's friendship that keeps us sane, don't you think? When all's said and done, it's our friends that really matter."

"I guess so," I said.

Her hand lingered on my shoulder, and she gazed at me in a way that made me nervous. "I don't mean to pry, baby," she said, "and it's probably just me, reading hardship into other people's lives because of the hardship in my own . . . but are you *sure* you're all right?"

"Well, yeah. Why?"

"It's just that you've seemed awfully down these last couple of weeks."

My fingers tightened on the cash bag.

"No doubt I'm butting my head in where I don't belong," she went on, "but I wondered if maybe it was your friend Kate. You used to talk about her all the time, Kate this and Kate that." She hesitated. "Have you two had a falling-out?"

Tears sprang to my eyes. My reaction was so unexpected that it made me light-headed.

"I'm fine," I said, blinking hard. "And Kate's fine, too."

"Truly?"

I nodded and made myself smile. Anyway, it was crazy for Darlin to be worrying about me, when her boyfriend had just dumped her. It was just wrong.

Darlin sighed. "You're a good person, Lissa. You deserve good things."

"You, too," I said weakly. I grabbed my walkie-talkie. "I better get going."

I had three back-to-back orders after delivering Mr. Rossey's shrimp scampi, and that was good because the fast pace helped me focus. Two of the orders went to Catherine Towers, a retirement complex that smelled like Clorox and cooked cabbage. No wonder so many of the residents ordered out. The first of the two went to Mrs. Babbits, who pressed a five-dollar tip into my hand and told me to be careful, the world was full of crazies. Her warning was fulfilled forty-five minutes later when I returned with Mrs. Gladstone's pasta with asparagus tips. I was flushed and out of breath when I knocked on her door—I'd jogged up two flights of stairs to get it to her since the elevator was slow, and I knew I was running late—and when Mrs. Gladstone saw me, she stepped back and wrinkled her nose.

"Young ladies are supposed to glow," she said disapprovingly. "I am afraid you have gone beyond the call."

I had no answer to that. On a previous visit Mrs. Gladstone

had told me about an exercise class she took called "Twinges in the Hinges," making pointed glances at my midsection as she extolled the benefits of a moderate aerobic workout. I'd seen her since in her exercise leotard and wraparound denim skirt, and she'd been wearing as much makeup as if she'd been returning from the theater instead of the gym. I'd imagined her in class, lazily rotating her feet and perhaps lifting a languid arm here and there. I doubted she'd ever perspired in her life.

"Here's your pasta," I said, lifting the Styrofoam box from my carrying case.

"Yes," she said, lifting the lid and peering at the asparagus. "I shall have fragrant urine all evening."

I pasted on a smile. How sweat could be considered more inappropriate than urine was beyond me. Mrs. Gladstone was a freak. All I could think as I got back in my truck was that if Kimberly had showed up at work on time, *she* could have been the one to hear about Mrs. Gladstone's urine instead of me. Or at least she'd have shared the load of deliveries, which would have kept me from running so late.

But Kimberly didn't log on until 6:35, a full hour after she was due to start.

"Breaker, breaker," she said, as I headed down Highland Avenue to Babette's Café. "Lissa, are you there? Over."

I picked up my walkie-talkie, feeling grouchy already. "I'm here. Over."

"Will you tell me again where Fellini's is? I think Darlin said Howell Mill and Northside. Is that right? Over."

I sighed. "No, it's Howell Mill and Collier." I gave her directions, the whole time thinking that she shouldn't have taken a delivery job unless she actually knew the city. Of course, I didn't know the city when I started either, but I got a map and figured it out on my own. I knew better than to bug anyone else with my problems.

"Ten-four," Kimberly said when I finished. "Thanks, good buddy. Over."

There was dead air for several minutes. The tension in my neck started to fade, and I began to think that maybe Kimberly was going to stick to her own deliveries and leave me alone. I was starting to feel the tiniest bit guilty, even, when my walkie-talkie buzzed and Kimberly's voice blared into the truck.

"So you know last time when we were talking about dreams?" she said. "Well, listen to what I dreamed last night. It was amazing. I dreamed I was a priestess, and serpents were winding their way up my arms, like those fortune-teller snakes from ancient Greece." She clicked off for a moment, then buzzed back on. "But it wasn't gross or anything. Do you think it sounds gross? Over."

I kept my eyes on the road. I was tempted to not even answer, but finally I grabbed the walkie-talkie and said, "Why are you telling me this? Over."

"Because you've got that book and everything. So what do you think it means? My dream, that is. Over."

"I have no idea. Over."

"We-l-l-l-l," she said, "priestesses from thousands of years ago really did wear snakes around their arms. And Jung says we all share the same basic memories. Do you think maybe that's what I'm tapping into? He says our psyches are made up of layers, like an onion, and the deeper you go, the closer you come to the core of human experience."

I exhaled through my nose. All I could think was, *an onion. I am being forced to talk to an onion.*

"Kimberly . . ." I said. I didn't go on—I didn't know how—and after a few seconds she took over.

"Um, actually, it's Ariel. Over."

"Excuse me?"

"My spiritual name. Remember?"

Anger lodged in my chest, and I jammed down the talk button. "Fine," I said. "But you know what? I don't care. And I don't want to hear about your dreams. I really don't." I braked hard to avoid rear-ending the Saab in front of me. "Over."

Silence filled the truck. My palms were damp, and my pulse thudded in my ears. I never went off on people like that. *Never.* And along with a rush of adrenaline, I felt queasy, like when I was little and I knew I'd done something wrong.

"Well, forgive me for trying to have a conversation," Kimberly—excuse me, *Ariel*—said at last. "Over."

I winced. I turned into the Babette's Café parking lot and cut off the engine, but I didn't get out of my seat. I waited in case she said anything else.

She didn't.

At the end of the night, I checked Darlin's driveway from the road before pulling in to drop off my stuff. No blue Volvo. Good. I hopped out of the truck and rapped on the door.

"Come on in," Darlin called. "Just leave your things on the table."

I stepped inside the entry hall. I heard bathwater running, then footsteps on the floor above me. Darlin poked her head over the balcony and said, "I am going to have a cup of tea and a nice cry. Ariel's suggestion. Doesn't that sound lovely?"

"I guess," I said. My stomach dipped because I was worried, with all the talk of crying, that she might ask more about me. But she didn't. I set my carrying case on the floor and lay the cash bag and the walkie-talkie on the table. "So she already checked in?"

"About fifteen minutes ago. Told me one man tipped her twenty dollars. Can you imagine?"

I narrowed my eyes. It figured that not only would she start late, but she'd find a way to finish first. *And* get phenomenal tips.

"Next time send me," I said. Darlin smiled, but I wasn't joking. I headed for the door, then stopped and turned around. My heart thumped, but I made myself ask. "You going to be okay? You want me to, I don't know, get you anything?"

"Thanks, baby," Darlin said. "But no. I just need to feel sorry for myself for a while."

"Well . . . all right. Good night."

"Good night, Lissa. You take care."

In the driveway, a dark shape moved in the shadows. Alarm shot through me, and then I saw who it was. "Jesus, Kimberly—*Ariel*—whatever the hell you want me to call you." I strode toward my truck. "What are you doing?"

"Relax," Ariel said. "I'm not trying to force you into a conversation, God forbid." She stepped closer, close enough for me to see the swirly purple skirt she wore over her red tights. Her hair sprouted from her head in two doggie-ears. "It's about Darlin."

"What about Darlin?"

"You know about Burl?" she said.

"Yes, I know about Burl." It pissed me off that she would even ask, as if she and Darlin were suddenly such good friends that Darlin would tell her something and not me.

"You know that Burl's family said Darlin was trying to fatten him up so that no other woman would want him?" Ariel asked.

She lifted her eyebrows, which I interpreted as smugness, and I said, "Burl's, what, in his forties? Why does he even care what his family thinks? Anyway, he's skinny as a stick. He's anemic."

"Doesn't matter. The point is, Darlin's depressed. I told her we'd take her out to cheer her up."

"*What?*"

"She didn't mention it? Figures. Probably assumed you wouldn't do it."

I started to speak, then stopped. I glared at her. Finally I said, "What is your *problem?*"

"*My* problem?" Ariel said. "Look. I suggested it *before* I started my deliveries, before I knew about your issues with the rest of humanity."

I protested, but she bulldozed over me.

"Darlin was depressed, and so I stayed and talked to her because I could tell she needed to. And I told her the three of us should go out, because otherwise she's just going to hole up in her house, and everything will be a million times worse." She put her hands on her hips. "I would have told you over the walkie-talkies, but I didn't want Darlin listening in and thinking we were gossiping about her."

I turned away. I was angry that Ariel had ambushed me like this, but I also felt bad that Ariel—and not me—had come up with a plan to cheer Darlin up. I'd wanted to do something for Darlin, but as usual, I didn't know how.

"She wouldn't have listened in," I said. "She never listens in."

Ariel shrugged.

I scowled. "So when is this big night supposed to happen? And why did you drag me into it?"

Ariel looked at me as if she couldn't believe I was such a jerk. "Because I thought you were her friend."

"I *am* her friend."

"Well, good. Because we're picking her up on Wednesday." Her eyes darted from mine, and she spoke quickly. "We're joining a singles' group called the Supper Club. I read about it in the weekend section of the paper. It's, uh, mainly for people over forty."

My mouth dropped open. "We're joining a . . . ?" I stared at her in disbelief. "Oh no we're not. *I'm* sure as hell not."

"See? I knew you wouldn't do it."

"A *singles'* group?"

"It's not for us. It's for Darlin."

"Oh yeah? And what does she say about this?"

Ariel fidgeted with the edge of her sweater. "She said, if you go, she'll go."

I barked out a laugh. "Well, Ariel, there's your answer. Darlin knew she was safe, because she knew I'd never agree."

"But I could tell she wanted to. She was just scared." She lifted her head, and her expression looked defiant, like a little kid's. "Don't you think sometimes you shouldn't do what you'd normally do? That maybe you should try something new?"

Something inside me flared up, then just as swiftly withdrew. I didn't know what I thought, other than that nothing was easy anymore and no matter what I did, things got messed up.

Ariel's face closed over. "Never mind. Just forget it."

"No. I'll do it. Fine." What did I care? My "normal" way of doing things sure wasn't getting me anywhere, so why not go on a group date with a slew of desperate forty-year-olds? It could hardly make things worse.

"Oh," Ariel said. "Well . . . that's great." Now that I'd agreed, she seemed unsure of how to act.

I frowned and climbed into the truck.

"Lissa," she said. She put her hand on the door.

"What?"

For a second she didn't say anything, and I exhaled impatiently. Color rose in her cheeks.

"That dream?" she said. "About the snakes?"

I looked at her like *you've got to be kidding.*

"No, wait, I'm not . . . I'm not trying to . . ." She closed her eyes. When she opened them, she said, "I made it up. I never dreamed I was a priestess. Okay?"

I pressed my tongue to the back of my teeth. Unbelievable. She was absolutely unbelievable.

"Right," I said, as if it were perfectly sane to force made-up dreams onto practically complete strangers. I closed the door, turned on the engine, and shifted into reverse. I knew I should say more, at least ask her why she would lie about something so dumb, but I no longer had the energy to care.

10

ON SUNDAY, I WENT BACK AND FORTH between feeling mad about the whole Ariel situation and feeling embarrassed about how I'd acted when I finally agreed to her plan. I *did* want to help cheer Darlin up, I really did, so why couldn't I have been more pleasant about it? But even when I felt embarrassed, I got mad, because it seemed lately as if my whole life revolved around feeling crappy for one reason or another.

I decided to take a nap, just to forget about it for a while. I shut my door and turned off the ringer on the phone. Not that I was expecting any calls, but if I were going to try to have a lucid dream, which right then I decided I was, I didn't want to risk interruptions.

I looked around my room, which was somewhat messy, but not too bad. I picked up a pair of sweatpants that I'd left on the floor and stuffed them in a drawer. On my dresser were several pairs of earrings, and I swept them into my palm and put them back in the stained-glass box where I kept my jewelry. I straightened a pile of books on my desk.

When there was nothing left to distract me, I kicked off my shoes and stretched out on my bed. The coolness of the quilt was soothing, but my body felt tight. I changed positions, but it didn't help. I was too wound up.

Last night I'd had that dream again, the one about being kidnapped. Only this time it was a girl who was luring me across the parking lot, instead of some strange man. It was a kid I used to know in elementary school, a girl named Cookie Churchill. In my dream it was sunny out, and everything was bright and shiny, and there was Cookie Churchill, smiling widely and beckoning with her hand. "Come on, Lissa," she said. "Come with me."

We walked past rows of parked cars, light glinting off the windows. Then we passed a station wagon, and alone all the way in the back was a little kid. She had her face pressed against the glass, and her expression was forlorn. I slowed down, and Cookie got impatient.

"Come *on*," she said. "She's fine. Do you think her mother would have left her if she wasn't fine?"

I'd woken up sweaty and disoriented. I hadn't thought about Cookie for years. Why the hell was I dreaming about her now?

Cookie and I had been friends in the third grade, although she was the kind of friend who was totally hot and cold. Some days she'd save me a swing and yell at anyone else who tried to take it, while on other days she'd make fun of my clothes, or my barrettes. Back then I wore those plastic ones with little animals on them. Cookie called them "baby bar-rettes."

Our friendship hadn't lasted long, and in sixth grade Cookie had moved to Chicago. So why, all these years later, was she pushing her way into my brain, especially in that one particular dream?

So do something about it, I told myself. *That's the point of this whole lucid-dreaming stuff—to quit being so powerless.*

I turned my thoughts to my dream book, recalling its suggestion to try to stay alert as I slipped from wakefulness to sleep. If I could build a bridge between consciousness and unconsciousness, the author said, then I could maintain awareness in my dreams. And once I knew how to maintain awareness, I could explore my dream life in any fashion I chose.

I closed my eyes and evened out my breathing, and eventually my mind slowed down. The goal now was to go ahead and fall asleep, but in a deliberate, purposeful way, so that I could focus on retaining my conscious awareness.

I began by tensing and relaxing my different muscle groups, and this time I remembered my stomach. It was still hard for me to actually sense a wave of energy moving through me, but I tried. When I finally got to the top of my head, I realized that I felt longer than I usually did. Not taller, but longer, more stretched out, like a piecrust rolled thinner and thinner. It was weird, but not a bad weird. It made me aware of my body in a different way.

The exercise was going well—no vibrating yet, but a light humming—so I took it to the next step. I imagined a ball of light moving from my head down to my feet, then around my body and back into my head. I exhaled and the cycle began again. The humming became a whole-body trembling.

I pushed on the feelings, like I did last time, and out of nowhere a wave of *desire* pulsed through me. Panic beat in my rib cage, and I braced myself against the sensation. Eventually it passed. And then my body gradually went numb, starting with my fingers and creeping up my arms to my spine. My heart pounded, but I hung on, telling myself everything was okay, I wasn't going to have a heart attack.

And then BANG.

I am outside. I am alone. The sky glows a deep, velvety blue, and an enormous moon looms above the trees. Everything looks more sharply defined than in the real world. I can see the air particles, I swear I can.

It lasted only an instant, and then I was back in bed. The house was quiet in a flat, familiar way, and my room was the same as ever. The only thing different was me. My body tingled, as if I'd dropped from a strange and wonderful world into this quite ordinary one.

I pushed myself up, blinking in the afternoon sun. What had just happened? It wasn't a lucid dream, at least not the way the book defined it, because I certainly hadn't been in control of what happened. If I didn't know better, I'd wonder if I'd had an out-of-body experience. That's what it felt like— as if I'd been flung out of my body and into a new realm altogether.

But I *did* know better. One thing my dream book taught me is that there's no such thing as an astral body that separates from your physical body and goes drifting off into space. Sometimes people think they've left their physical bodies, but that's just their brains' way of dealing with the vividness of the dream. The experience feels so real that people assume it *is* real, and their brains, whose job it is to process information, come up with the best explanation they can: they've had an out-of-body experience. Or astrally projected themselves. Or whatever.

I thought it was interesting how the brain worked that way, how it went to such lengths to make things fit with prior experience. It reminded me of the time I'd gone to the beach with Kate's family, when I'd spent an entire morning searching for sand dollars. For the longest time I couldn't find any, because I was used to seeing nothing but sand, and so that's all I was able to see. But once I found my first sand dollar, I was able to find them everywhere. I just had to develop a new way of seeing.

That's what I had to do now, only with dreaming instead of seeing. Next time, if there was a next time, I had to remember that I hadn't really left my body, even if that's what it felt like. Once I could accept the fact that I was actually dreaming, even if it *felt* like I was awake, then I could enter fully into the dream and explore it intentionally. At least, that was my hope.

I drew my legs to my chest and thought again about what had just happened. Whatever else it was, it wasn't a *normal* dream, that's for sure. Which meant that maybe I was making progress. Who knows?

I rested my cheek on my knees, letting the memory of the dream wash over me. I'd never seen a moon like that in my life.

CHAPTER 11

IT OCCURRED TO ME, THE NEXT DAY AT LUNCH, that maybe my moon dream *was* a lucid dream after all.

"Mashed potatoes?" the woman behind the counter asked.

"Huh? Oh. Yes, please." It *had* to be, because it had the same larger-than-life quality as the dreams described in my book, the same feeling of *wow, this is totally incredible.*

"Carrots?"

"No, thanks."

She handed me my plate, and I picked up my tray and headed for a vacant table at the far end of the cafeteria. So all I had to do, I concluded, was figure out how to stay in that strange dream state long enough to control it. And I could do that. Right now, with the buzz of excitement giving me a rush, all sorts of things felt possible.

"Hey! Lissa! Over here!"

I turned. It was Kimberly/Ariel, gesturing to the empty seat beside her. Or rather, to the many empty seats beside her. The only other person at her table was Finn O'Connor, a guy I vaguely knew but had never really talked to.

I hesitated, and Ariel's expression changed. I could tell she regretted calling out to me, and I couldn't blame her. The wonder of it was that she kept trying at all.

A group of girls brushed past me, chatting loudly as they ambled toward their table. Not one of them looked my way. I squared my shoulders and strode across the room, telling myself that surely I could put up with Ariel for half an hour.

"Hi," I said, nodding to her and Finn.

"Hi," Ariel said. She took a sip of iced tea. "I was just telling Finn about Entrées on Trays, which, I've decided, is my favorite job of all time. Did I tell you I got a twenty-dollar tip last time?"

Her tone was light. She was pretending everything was normal between us.

I unloaded my tray and said, "Darlin mentioned it. Way to go." I smiled, determined to be nice if it killed me.

"Darlin's the owner?" Finn asked. "The one you're going clubbing with?"

My smile froze.

"Not *clubbing*," Ariel said. She gave me a nervous grin. "We're taking her out, that's all."

"Going to wear your gold lamé?"

"Ha, ha, Lissa knows you're kidding. Right, Lissa?"

I buttered my roll, telling myself to relax. So what if Finn knew I was joining a forties-and-over singles' group? Who honestly cared? I took in Ariel's gauzy blouse and thick eyeliner, the silver hoop in her nose, and I said, "So, at school, do you still want me to call you—"

"Ariel," she finished. "Absolutely. Hey, I like that: Absolutely Ariel."

"You know, you're just encouraging her," Finn said to me. "First the name change, now the nightclub—oh, and did she tell you her I-am-an-ancient-priestess dream?"

I blinked. What was it with her and this ludicrous dream, the one she hadn't even actually had? I felt a stab of sympathy for her, which surprised me.

"She did," I said. "Pretty interesting, huh?"

He snorted. "I'll say."

Ariel shot me a look of gratitude, then crumpled her napkin into a ball and threw it at Finn. "Do not make light of the divine. That was a very revealing dream."

"My point exactly."

Ariel's gaze shifted, and she nodded toward the front of the room. Hey," she said, "isn't that your friend Kate?"

I glanced up. There she was, walking out of the food line. Her hair was held back in a loose French twist, and she wore a faded denim shirt with the sleeves rolled up. She looked beautiful.

"Kate!" Ariel called out. "Over here!"

I grabbed her arm. "Ariel, stop!"

"What? You don't want her to sit with us?"

I dropped her arm and hunched lower in my seat. Kate had turned and was heading our way.

"You guys have a fight or something?" Ariel said. "You're all pale. What's the matter?"

"Nothing," I said. "Shut up. Please."

Kate stood in front of us. She glanced from me to Ariel, then back to me. "Hi," she said.

I swallowed. "Hi."

"What's up?"

I didn't respond. I wasn't trying to be a jerk. In fact, I was making a deliberate effort *not* to be a jerk, even though every muscle in my body had gone stiff the moment she approached. But I couldn't find it in me to make polite chitchat, either. There was just no way.

Beside me, Ariel wound a strand of hair around her finger. She'd planned on asking Kate to sit with us, I guess, but now she didn't know what to do. "Nice necklace," she finally said. "The turquoise matches your shirt."

My eyes dropped to Kate's neck, the hollow above her collarbone.

"Thanks," Kate said. "My boyfriend gave it to me."

I looked away.

Kate waited a few more seconds. "Well, I'm going to go eat. My food's getting cold."

"So go," I said. It came out before I could think.

She exhaled. "Lissa."

I blushed and stabbed at my mashed potatoes.

"We need to talk," she said. Her eyes darted to Ariel and Finn, and she lowered her voice. "Call me. Okay?" She paused, searching my face, then pressed her lips together and walked to the other side of the cafeteria, where she sat down with Ben and some of his friends. Ben tucked a strand of hair behind her ear, and she cast a nervous look in my direction. Then she leaned toward Ben and said something that made him laugh.

"God, she's gorgeous," Ariel said. "If I were a guy, I would have *such* a crush on her."

I pulled my fork out of my mashed potatoes, wiped it on the side of my plate, and cut a bite of meat loaf, trimming the edges so it was a perfect square.

"Is that her boyfriend? Ben Porter? He looks full of himself. Is he, or is he a nice guy?"

I shrugged.

Ariel tipped back her chair. "I mean, God, her hair. I would *kill* for hair like that."

"What, so you could dye it purple?" Finn said. He glanced at me. "I've always liked brown hair. It seems more real."

I cut the square into four smaller squares.

Ariel leaned forward so that the front legs of her chair banged on the floor. She rapped the table with her knuckles. "Hey! You going to eat that meat loaf or play with it?" She laughed. "Ha. I sound like my grandmother."

I put down my knife and fork. I made myself smile. "So, uh, have you told Finn about all of that collective unconscious stuff? How our psyches have layers, like an onion?"

"Yes, I have, and shut up, Finn, because Carl Jung is not some crackpot and you know it." She tore off a bite of roll and stuffed it in her mouth. "Jung also says that ignoring your dreams is like ignoring your shadow, and that people who refuse to embrace their shadows are doomed to be incomplete. What do you think of that, Mr. Too-Cool-for-School?"

Finn laughed. "I think that anyone who tries to embrace his shadow is going to end up with a broken nose."

"Not your real shadow, dummy. Your symbolic shadow." She leaned forward. "Your *dark* side."

"Lissa?" Finn said. "Do you have a *dark* side?"

He used the same intonation as Ariel, and I knew he was

joking. Still, I busied myself with my potatoes. "Hey, don't talk to me about it. Ariel's the one with the answers."

Ariel whacked her forehead. "Shit. Speaking of answers, I've got to get my French done before next period. Shit, shit, shit." She stood up and lifted her tray. "You guys coming?"

"Yeah," I said. I reached for my napkin, then drew back, confused. What startled me was Finn's hand, hanging by his side as he stood up. His right hand was normal, but his left hand was tiny. Like a baby's, almost.

He caught me staring and juggled his tray so that the left side was propped on his forearm, hiding his hand from view. His neck and face flushed red.

Silently, I followed them to the side of the cafeteria where we dumped our trash. It was obviously some kind of birth defect, Finn's hand. How had I not seen it until now? He kept it in his lap during lunch; that's why I didn't see it while we were talking. But I'd been in school with him since we were freshmen. Two years.

You'd think you would notice something like that. If someone were that different, you'd think everyone would know.

12

BETH AND VANESSA WERE IN THE DEN when I got home, watching a soap opera and eating Doritos. On the soap, a woman snooped around in somebody's room, and Vanessa explained that Evelyn—that was the woman's name—was searching for her ex-husband's checkbook to see if he'd made a purchase at Victoria's Secret recently.

"Evelyn's still in love with Vance," Vanessa said, "but Vance is in love with Jewel, Evelyn's sister. Yesterday Jewel wore this sexy nightgown that Evelyn *knew* Vance had given her, so now she's trying to prove it."

"Oh," Beth said.

"Hi, Beth," I said. "Hi, Vanessa."

"Hi," they said, eyes glued to the screen. Evelyn found the checkbook and flipped through it, lips parted in concentration. "That bastard!" she cried. She hurled the checkbook at the mirror and burst into tears.

"Why aren't you watching the Cartoon Network?" I asked.

Beth turned to me and glared. "This is better. Shh."

I went into the kitchen to get a snack. When I passed back through with a Coke and a handful of M&M's, a dark-haired woman was locked in an embrace with an older man.

"Oh, my darling," Vanessa mimicked, drawing her hand to her chest and batting her eyelashes at Beth.

Beth giggled. "Oh, Jewel, you are so passionate."

Vanessa heaved a sigh. "Kiss me, Vance. Kiss me this instant."

Still giggling, Beth leaned in closer, her lips grazing Vanessa's cheek.

"Ew!" Vanessa cried. "Not really, you lesbo!"

I set my jaw and strode through the room. I was trying to like Vanessa, but it was hard. Besides, I hated that word, *lesbo*. Last year, or even last month, I'd have gotten up on a soapbox if I'd heard Vanessa say that, telling her how wrong it was to make fun of being gay, blah, blah, blah. Now the last thing I wanted to do was make a big deal over it, and my face burned as if *I* were the one who'd done something.

But I didn't think being gay was *wrong*. Did I?

One of Jerry's frequent customers was gay. Her name was Heather, and I knew she was gay because she told me and Jerry about the commitment ceremony she'd had with her partner last New Year's Eve. Her partner's name was Katrina. Heather acted like it was perfectly normal that she loved another woman, and I'd felt all proud of myself for treating it that way, too. And no, I *didn't* think there was anything wrong with a woman loving another woman, or a man loving another man. Deep down, I knew I didn't. But it was one thing for someone else to be gay. It was something else entirely if that person was me.

Maybe it was better once you were an adult, although even then I was sure you'd run into people who didn't understand. But in high school? God. If the kids I knew found out two girls were into each other, they'd treat them like pariahs. Not all the kids, but enough. And guys like Travis Wyrick would go nuts, tossing out insults and calling them "dykes." Or making jokes about forming a sex triangle, if the girls were pretty.

My cheeks were still hot, even though I was alone in my room. I hated how edgy I felt, how all of a sudden I was afraid of my own emotions. And I hated that I had no one to talk to about it. I wrapped my arms around my ribs, my body tight with anxiety.

Once upon a time I could have talked to Kate, and once upon a time she would have listened. And the ironic thing was the two of us *did* talk about being gay once, before things got so screwed up. It was during one of our late-night conversations up in her room, me on one twin bed and her on the other. It was so dark that we couldn't see each other. We could only hear each other's voices.

"In some ways I bet it would be really nice," Kate had said. "You know? I think about how much closer I am to you than I am to my guy friends, and I wonder if that's what it's like. Like, you'd understand everything the other person was going through, and you'd take such good care of each other. Not like when you go out with a guy and he dumps you for a football game or something."

"I know what you mean," I said, although really I didn't. Having boyfriend after boyfriend was Kate's scene, not mine.

"Although I'm sure gay couples have problems, too. But maybe they're able to talk about them more easily."

"Maybe. I guess it just depends. But think about it: if you were dating a girl, you'd have so much in common. You'd like the same kinds of books, the same kinds of movies—God, no more Jackie Chan!"

"Or John Wayne," I groaned. In ninth grade, Kate had dragged me with her on an absurdly bad double date to a Western film festival. It was torture.

Kate laughed. "Seriously. You could see all the chick flicks you wanted, one after another, with a huge bowl of popcorn and a box of Kleenex."

For a while neither of us spoke. I thought Kate had fallen asleep—she did that sometimes, just dozed off in the middle of a conversation—but then I heard her roll over so she was facing me. "What about the physical part?" she asked.

"What do you mean?"

"You know."

"It's . . . kind of hard to imagine, isn't it?"

"Yeah. I mean, what do they *do*, exactly?"

Both of us were silent.

"It might not be so bad . . ." Kate started.

I stared through the dark at the ceiling. "I don't know. Maybe kind of soft? And just, you know, comfortable?"

"While at the same time wildly passionate and hot, hot, hot," Kate said. She giggled. "I mean, come on. *You* know where everything is, *she* knows where everything is . . ." Her tone changed. "But see, that's how I know I'm not gay. I'm not attracted to girls like I am to guys. I'm just not."

"Well, yeah," I had said. I'd felt confused, as if I'd been scolded for something I hadn't done. "Same here."

I thought of that now, and I closed my eyes. A whisper in my mind quickened my pulse: *Please, God, don't let it be me.*

Later, after Vanessa went home and we'd eaten dinner, Beth found me in the kitchen and stood around doing nothing until I looked up from my calculus.

"What?" I said.

She traced the pattern of the linoleum with her toe. "What's a *lesbo?*"

I put down my pencil. "Vanessa shouldn't have called you that."

"Is it a bad word?"

"No. Well, sort of."

"Why? What does it mean?"

"It's short for *lesbian.* Do you know what a lesbian is?"

She nodded, then shook her head.

"A lesbian's a woman who loves other women." I picked up my pencil and bent over my work.

Beth shifted her weight to her other foot. "What do you mean, loves other women?"

"What do you mean, what do I mean? If you're a lesbian, then you love women instead of men. You're attracted to them, you want to be with them. But you're not a lesbian, Beth, so don't worry about it."

"Is it the same as being gay?"

"I *said* don't worry about it." I could hear how sharp my voice was. "Now leave me alone. I've got to finish this."

Beth watched me for a couple of seconds, then turned and went into the den. Two minutes later she came back. "So how do you know if you're a lesbian?"

87

"Jesus, Beth. How am I supposed to know? You wake up with a big, red L stamped on your forehead. You crop your hair and stop shaving your legs."

She stared at me, and I gathered my books and stormed past her. My breathing felt off, as if not enough air was reaching my lungs. I paused at the bottom of the staircase, chest tight. I heard Beth's footsteps, and I hurried up the stairs.

13

SOMETHING IS ON TOP OF ME, *squishing me, and I jerk away so violently that I roll off the bed and onto the floor. I open my eyes and I see the bed above me, the covers sliding off in a tangled heap. But something's not right. The sheets, why are they orange? And why are they so fuzzy?*

"Wait," I tell myself. "Just wait. It's because you're dreaming."

Omigod, I'm dreaming!

I lift myself off the floor—easily, like a puff of air.

I float out of my bedroom and into the hall, past Beth's cracked-open door and down the staircase. I can see every grain of wood on the handrail, every fleck of paint on the walls. I propel myself toward the wide kitchen window above the sink, but I bump against the pane and bounce back. I back up and try again, focusing my concentration, and this time I push through—ZIP—like pushing through steam.

In front of the house, I see a girl walking down the street. My spine tingles, because it's late. She shouldn't be out by herself.

"Hey," I say, but the girl doesn't look up. "Excuse me," I say louder.

I float closer and I see the girl's face: it's Kate. She doesn't notice that I'm hovering in front of her. She doesn't hear me when I call her name.

"Kate!" I cry. I wave my hand in front of her face.

I don't like this. I want to wake up . . .

I'm in the bathroom, flossing my teeth. The light on the tiles is harsh and yellow. I put down the floss and lean forward, peering at my reflection in the mirror. My eyes—there's something different about my eyes. They're brown, but underneath the brown is a luminous gold that pulses as I breathe.

I hear a noise. I turn my head, and SNAP! I have returned.

I sat up, flipping on the lamp on my bedside table. At first I was too confused to think straight. Why was I in bed? Why wasn't I on the floor? And then I realized—omigod! I did it! I had another lucid dream, and this time I stayed in it long enough to actually make things happen!

I looked down at my sheets, grabbing handfuls of the smooth fabric. How weird to dream of fuzzy orange sheets. But before that—it was coming back—I'd been dreaming something upsetting, something about being smothered. And in my dream, I pulled away so hard that I rolled off the bed. Although obviously I didn't really roll off the bed, because here I was still in bed. But in the dream I looked up and saw those crazy sheets, which were so clearly *not* my sheets that I was jarred out of my "normal" dream into a lucid dream.

I wiggled my feet under the covers. This was huge!

Okay. So after I realized I was dreaming, I lifted myself up and floated around the house. God, was that wild.

Then I'd drifted downstairs and out the kitchen window.

And then—what next?

Oh.

I drew my knees to my chest, remembering the part about Kate and the deserted street. How she couldn't see me even though I was right there in front of her. God. I spent most of my waking life trying *not* to think about her. Why did she have to show up in my dreams?

And then there was that weird part about my eyes, when I *thought* I woke up but was actually still dreaming. A false awakening—that was the term my book used. The author said it was a good thing, a way to prolong lucidity. Maybe so, but it was eerie.

I shivered. My closet door was open a crack, and I had the old urge to cross the room and shut it. As a kid, I had to check under the bed and in the closet at least two times before turning out my bedside light. Jerry thought I was crazy.

I padded down the hall to Beth's room. She was curled on her side, one hand tucked beneath her cheek and the other in a loose fist under her chin. Her lips were open and a tiny bit of spit glistened at the corner of her mouth. I loved her all the time, but I especially loved her when she was sleeping. She looked so innocent.

I brushed a piece of hair off her face. She didn't move. I shook her shoulder, and this time she stirred under the covers. I stepped away and stole back to my room.

A minute later she tiptoed across my floor and swayed by

the side of my bed. "Lissa?" she mumbled. "Can I sleep with you?"

"Beth," I chided, although this was why I woke her up.

"Please?"

"Oh, all right." I scooted over to make room for her, and she climbed in beside me.

"Want me to scratch your back?" she said.

"That's okay. Just go back to sleep."

Her breathing grew steady, and her small body warmed her side of the bed. I pulled the quilt around the two of us and tried to recapture my earlier excitement. *I did it,* I told myself again. *I had a lucid dream.*

It didn't have quite the same punch.

Still, the knowledge of what I'd done stayed with me. Like an underground stream. A promise.

CHAPTER 14

CALL ME, KATE HAD SAID. And I wanted to. I dialed the first six digits of her number, then clutched the phone for what seemed like forever, finger hovering above the 2 until the system disconnected.

We need to talk.

I was desperate to talk. Didn't she know that? Didn't she know how much I missed her, how much I missed just hanging out with her? Didn't she miss it, too?

She used to say I was the only person she really trusted, that she could tell me things she had never told another soul. Like the fact that she peed in her pants when she laughed too hard, or that she hated to wear sandals because she thought her toes were too hairy. Hobbit feet, she called them. And once she told me how she could hear her parents having sex from her bedroom, even with the door shut and the stereo on. "It's just *wrong,*" she said, lowering her voice even though no one was near.

I'd laughed and said she should be glad her parents had sex, period. And I reassured her about the other stuff, too, reminding her that everybody had some weird body thing they were embarrassed about. "Anyway, your toes are perfect," I told her.

She leaned against me. "You're so full of it, Lissa. You know that, don't you?"

But now Kate had Ben, who, to tell the truth, *was* pretty full of himself. Like that night at Rob's house when he stood on top of the pool table and proclaimed that he was the ruler of the universe. Yeah, he was drunk, and yeah, he was kidding, but still, it takes a certain arrogance to say something like that in the first place. And the cigar. God. High school guys should not smoke cigars, just as high school guys should not attempt to grow facial hair. Give it a rest.

That was the night Kate and Ben first hooked up, after the guys started smoking cigars and after Kate and I fled to the gazebo, laughing, to escape. We made fun of how cool they thought they were, and how Rob, the first time he inhaled, practically coughed up his entire lung. "And Ben," Kate scoffed. "I'm sorry, but lose the ponytail, okay, guy? He looks like one of those investment bankers who wears his hair long to make a ridiculous stab at being hip. You *know* he's going to grow up to be some suit-wearing asshole who talks on his cell phone all the time."

"While smoking a cigar," I added.

By the end of the night, Kate and Ben were falling all over each other on the sofa while the others played quarters and I stood by myself at the door. She didn't notice when

I left. And even though almost a month had passed, it still made me feel alone.

Wednesday night, Ariel and I met at Darlin's for our big date. Our group date. Jesus. I felt resentful despite my resolve to make the best of it, and Ariel's enthusiasm only made matters worse.

"Excited?" she asked as she rapped on Darlin's door. She wore a pale blue dress that probably came from a thrift store, and her hair was held back with sparkly butterfly clips. She actually looked good in a hippie-chick kind of way, and I wondered if I should have worn something besides jeans and my gray sweatshirt.

"I hope she's not too nervous," she went on, her fingers flitting down the front of her dress. "I mean, not that there's anything to be nervous about, but . . . you know. It's always hard meeting new people."

Her eyes widened as if she'd said more than she meant to. An awkward silence hovered between us, and finally she knocked again on the door. "Darlin? You there?"

Darlin opened the door. She wore a flowing orange dress and orange sandals, and her face was heavily made up. "Well, ladies?" she said. She picked up her skirt with one hand and twirled around.

"You look great," I said.

"Yeah," Ariel said. "I love your dress."

"Well, I aim to please," Darlin said. "Orange is the color of communication, you know. Lets people know you're feeling social."

"Really?" Ariel said. She fingered her own dress. "What about blue? What does blue mean?"

"Navy blue hints at mystery, but a light blue like yours indicates playfulness." Darlin brushed a speck off Ariel's shoulder. "You look delightful, my dear."

"Why, thank you," Ariel replied. As we got into Ariel's car—Darlin in the front with Ariel, me in the back—she asked, "What do you wear if you're not feeling social? Black?"

"Heavens, yes. Just think of those dreadful New Yorkers."

"Yeah?" She kept her tone innocent. "What about gray?"

"Well, now. Someone wears gray when she's not sure what she's feeling—isn't that right, Lissa?" She caught my eye in the rearview mirror. "Only I suspect that most people who wear gray have a secret spot of orange hidden within."

"Oh, definitely," I said. I said it sarcastically, and Ariel and Darlin laughed.

At the Lone Star Steakhouse and Saloon, where the singles' group was meeting, Darlin's bravado disappeared. She drummed her fingers on the car door and said, "Now, girls, really, I am so honored to be out with you. Why not make it a girls' night out—my treat? The Cheesecake Factory's not five blocks down the road."

"It's just a bunch of people having dinner," Ariel said, releasing her seat belt. "If it helps, imagine them all in their underwear."

Darlin snorted. "Gracious, Ariel, I most certainly will not. What if they imagined me in *my* underwear?"

At which point I couldn't help but do exactly that. Ariel must have, too, because she looked at me and giggled.

"*Girls,*" Darlin said. She burst out laughing and leaned

back against her seat. "What in heaven's name have you two gotten me into?"

Inside, it was cool and dim. Bowls of peanuts sat on every table, and empty shells crunched under our shoes as we followed the hostess through the restaurant. From a silver jukebox blared the chorus of "I've Got Friends in Low Places." The hostess led us to a table in the corner, and Ariel stepped forward.

"Hi," she said. "Is this the Supper Club?"

Six heads turned toward us, and six voices rose in greeting. Everyone seemed to be middle-aged, if not older, and everyone seemed alarmingly friendly, calling out "Sure is," and "Hey there," and "Sit down. Take a load off!"

Other customers looked our way, and the muscles at the back of my neck bunched up. The ride over had been more fun than I'd expected, and for a brief moment I'd wondered if this outing might not be so bad after all. But as everyone introduced themselves, I had to fight not to bolt. I knew it was wrong of me, but I felt embarrassed to be here. I did not want to grow up to be an over-the-hill lonelyheart.

"We're real glad to have you," said the man at the end of the table. Phil, I think his name was. "Starr, if you scoot over a tad, these fine people can get situated."

Darlin squeezed past Starr and dropped into the one empty seat. "Whew," she said, smiling and fanning herself with a menu.

Ariel pulled up a chair from a nearby table. "So," she said, plunking her forearms on the table and addressing the entire group. "You're probably wondering why I asked you all here tonight."

Everyone laughed, Darlin the loudest of all and, in fact, *too* loudly. I pulled up a chair for myself and forced a smile.

"Just kidding," Ariel said. "But really, I think it's so cool that y'all do this, that you meet for dinner at all these different restaurants. You should ask Darlin for recommendations. She knows every single restaurant in Atlanta."

"Ariel—" Darlin protested.

Ariel waved her off. "She does. It's her job."

"That right?" Phil asked. "What do you do?"

A woman wearing huge round glasses leaned forward. "Are you a food critic? I think it would be so fun to be a food critic."

Darlin blushed. "It's nothing, really. I run a delivery service for upscale Atlanta restaurants. Entrées on Trays?"

"Entrées on Trays!" said the man sitting across from me. "I've seen your menus. I've been meaning to call."

"Well, please do," Darlin said. She explained to the others how it worked, and they nodded and asked questions, splintering off into discussions of this or that restaurant.

As they chatted, I studied them from under my bangs. Phil, the man sitting closest to Darlin, was a big guy with a receding hairline and smooth, soft skin. On Darlin's other side was Starr, who had bottle-blond hair and clumpy black eyelashes. Starr modeled for car ads; I knew because at one point she mentioned that Hooters had the best wings in the state and that her "boys" took her there whenever they finished a shoot. It wasn't hard to imagine her in a bikini and high heels, draped across a glossy red Mustang.

Next to Starr was Shawanna, an older black woman wearing navy slacks and a white blouse. She held herself properly—chin up, spine straight—and I got the feeling that she didn't quite approve of Starr, although she tried not to let it show.

And then there was a man who sold computers—Dave—and next to him a quiet man with tired eyes. I think his name was Scott. And finally the woman with the glasses. Her name was Gloria, and I could smell her perfume from across the table.

All of the members of the group seemed nice enough, but if so, then why were they here? What was wrong with them that they couldn't find a date on their own?

I was ashamed of myself for being so judgmental, but still, I wanted to leave. Especially since Darlin, full into the swing of a lively sushi-versus-sashimi debate, seemed oblivious to my presence. Sure, she'd been nervous at first, but anyone seeing her now would assume she was one of the gang.

And that was as disturbing as anything else. I didn't want to think of Darlin as part of this gang. I didn't want to think of myself as part of this gang, yet here I was as well. I pressed my heels into the floor and edged my chair away from the table.

"Phil, you devil," Darlin said, leaning forward in a way that revealed the tops of her freckled breasts. "Raw fish is not in the same category as oysters, thank you very much. Just because I enjoy my sushi does not make me the queen of love."

Phil laughed, a broad guffaw that brought more stares from the other customers. "If you say so, Darlin. But I've eaten plenty of sushi myself, and it sets my fin a'spinnin', if you get my drift."

"Oh, you are *bad*," Darlin said. She gave him a playful shove, and I winced. I glanced at Ariel, but she giggled along with Phil as if he were the funniest man on the planet.

"Y'all ready to order?" asked a waitress, stopping next to my chair and flipping open a leather pad.

No one responded. The waitress shifted her gaze to a neighboring table, where four college guys flirted with another server. She turned back and sighed. "Excuse me. Ex*cuse* me?"

"You guys," I said.

"Oh," Ariel said. She raised her voice over the din of the conversation. "Hey, is everyone ready to order?"

The waitress stood there as the others discussed drinks and appetizers, salads versus soups. I could read her thoughts by the way she held her mouth, and I smiled apologetically. *I'm not really with them*, I wanted to say. She stared right through me. I mumbled my order and handed over my menu.

Later, after Darlin downed two Peach Fizzies and everyone else had drunk their fair share of wine, beer, and, in Starr's case, tequila shooters with slices of lime, Phil suggested a line dance.

"We'll cut the rug with the Boot Scoot Boogie," he said, slapping the table and standing up. "What do you say, Darlin?"

Darlin tilted her glass and drank the slushy remains of her drink. "Oh, why not," she said. "Come on, girls!"

Ariel pushed back her chair, along with Gloria and a giggling Starr.

"What the hell," said Dave, lumbering to his feet. Scott shrugged and followed.

Shawanna and I were the only ones who stayed seated.

"I never have been good at those things," Shawanna said, fidgeting with her necklace. "You and me—we can just watch, right?"

Darlin sashayed to our end of the table. "Lissa, honey," she sang. She beckoned me with her finger.

"Come on, you two," Ariel said.

"You go ahead," I said.

Ariel clasped her palms. "Please?"

I waved her on, and Shawanna gave me a grateful smile. Together, we looked out at the dance floor. Dave was surprisingly graceful as he sauntered forward and stomped his foot, and Starr had this thing going with her hips that was an absolute riot, as Darlin would say. And Darlin herself was having a blast, swishing her skirt and shimmying when she did her quarter-turn. My chest loosened. From twenty feet away, I found it easier to feel tolerant of them all.

Burl, eat your heart out, I thought.

And then there was Ariel, who knew every step perfectly. She and Scott grinned as they moved in sync: heel to toe, heel to toe. I watched with grudging respect, realizing that she didn't have to work at acting natural, she just *was*. Or maybe it was just that she was as much of a misfit as the rest of them, so of course she felt right at home.

But that wasn't fair. I actually wished I were more like Ariel in some ways, more willing to go ahead and be weird if I wanted to. Or not even weird—just less self-conscious. I hated how self-conscious I felt all the time.

I took in Ariel's sweaty face and sensed something shift within me. It took guts for her to keep reaching out to me, unencouraged and uninvited. Plus, and I needed to remember this, it wasn't as if tons of others were waiting in line to take her place.

And really, I knew that Ariel wasn't so bad.

She just wasn't Kate.

15

FOR THE REST OF THE WEEK, I couldn't shake the thought that things between Kate and me were going to get patched up. I'd done a good and unselfish thing—I'd escorted Darlin on her date with the wild and crazy members of the Supper Club—and now I should be rewarded. Kate should call me.

Anytime now, she surely would.

So on Saturday morning, when Beth stuck her head into the bathroom and said the phone was for me, my heart sped up.

"Who is it?" I said, pulling back the shower curtain.

"I don't know. Jerry answered."

Jerry would know if it was Kate, at least I think he would. But that didn't mean he'd mention it to Beth. I turned off the water, grabbed a towel, and hurried to my room.

"Hello?" I said. To Jerry I called, "I've got it!"

"Hello, Lissa? It's Ariel."

"Ariel." I sat down on the bed, making a wet splotch on the quilt. "What's up?"

"Finn and I are going to IHOP for breakfast. Want to come?"

I closed my eyes.

"No line dancing, I promise," she said.

"I can't. I just got out of the shower."

"So put on some clothes. Or come naked. Hell, Finn would love it." She giggled. "We'll be there in twenty minutes, okay?"

I opened my eyes. I could go with Ariel and Finn or I could sit in my room, waiting for a call that was never going to come. "Sure," I said. "Why not."

The IHOP was a madhouse: kids screaming for juice, truckers eating platters of eggs and sausage, up-all-nighters staring bleary-eyed at their menus and laughing over nothing. There was a forty-five-minute wait to be seated, but Ariel knew one of the waitresses, and she squeezed us in at the next available table.

"Friends in high places," Ariel said. She shook her napkin into her lap. "I know everyone at Baskin-Robbins, too. You want a big scoop, you come with me."

"You want a big scoop, you come with me," Finn repeated, lowering his voice and glowering. He switched back to his normal self. "You sound like you're in the Mafia."

Ariel grinned. "You know it."

A five-year-old in the booth behind us whizzed a slice of orange at Finn's head, then slid out of sight. Finn picked up the orange slice, reached over the top of the booth, and tapped the kid's shoulder. "Excuse me," he said. "I think you dropped this."

"George!" the boy's mother said. "I told you to stop that!"

Finn looked at me and arched his eyebrows. "You, too, Lissa. No more roughhousing in the booth, you hear?"

I half-smiled, then returned to my menu. I shouldn't have come. I felt dull and sluggish.

"Y'all know what you want?" our waitress asked, setting a glass of water by each of our place mats.

I shut the menu. "A short stack of pancakes and a small orange juice, please."

"Same for me," Finn said.

"Wimps," Ariel said. She handed her menu to the waitress. "I'll have the chocolate-chip waffle with whipped cream and sprinkles."

"Want any sugar with that?" Finn said.

Ariel ignored him. "And a large orange juice. Thanks, Christina." She propped her elbows on the table and cupped her chin in her palms. "So. Guess what I've decided to be when I get out of school?"

"A dentist?" Finn said.

"No."

"A bunny rabbit?"

"*No*, a dowser. Wouldn't that be awesome?"

Finn turned to me. "A dowser. What's a dowser?"

I roused myself from my apathy. "Um, I'm not sure. Someone who finds things underground?"

"Not 'things,'" Ariel said. "Water. I'd use one of those Y-shaped rods and find water for people."

"Because so many people have lost their water," Finn said.

She rolled her eyes. "For wells, dummy."

"Oh, right. For wells." He leaned back in his seat "Lissa, do you have a well?"

"You know, we don't, actually. We've got a water pipe, although sometimes we misplace it . . ."

Finn laughed. I was pleased despite myself.

"Okay, fine," Ariel said. "But in Vermont and Connecticut there is a big business of well digging, and dowsers do really well. Ha! *Well*, get it?" She slapped the table. "Anyway, it would be a great way for me to stay in touch with Mother Earth and all that. Doesn't that sound fabulous?"

"How do you become a dowser?" I asked.

"That part I don't know yet," she admitted. "But how hard can it be?"

Finn and I looked at each other across the table.

Ariel launched into a pro/con analysis of metal dowsing rods versus wooden ones, stopping for breath only when Christina arrived with our food. Christina served Finn and me our pancakes, then placed Ariel's waffle before her with a flourish. On top of the waffle she'd squirted a whipped cream smiley-face, with a cherry for the nose and two chunks of pineapple for the eyes. "Thought I'd have a little fun with it. What do you think?"

Ariel clapped her hands. "Christina, I love it."

The five-year-old peered at Ariel's waffle over the top of the booth.

"Jealous, aren't you?" Finn said.

"Let me know if you need anything else," Christina said. She winked and headed to the kitchen.

"I think we should say a blessing," Ariel said.

"I think we shouldn't," Finn said.

Ariel held out her hands, one to each of us. When neither of us responded, she held them out farther, fingers wiggling. Finn groaned and took one hand. Reluctantly, I took the other.

Closing her eyes, Ariel chanted, "Thank you, Inanna, for the bounty you have spread before us. When we eat of this food, we eat of your body. Amen."

"Who's Inanna?" Finn said.

"An ancient goddess from Mesopotamia," Ariel said. She cut off a bite of waffle and popped it into her mouth. "People prayed to her by baking these special cakes which they placed on her altar. They called them 'cakes from heaven,' and when they ate them, it was like they were eating Inanna's own body."

"Clever," Finn said.

"Like communion?" I asked. My heaviness, without my realizing it, had begun to lift. "You know, when you eat the body of Christ?"

"Exactly," Ariel said, pointing her fork at me in approval. "Do you go to church?"

"I used to go with Kate sometimes. When we were in junior high, her mom would make us go."

"Is Kate Catholic?"

I shook my head. "Presbyterian."

"Grape juice, huh? If you're Catholic, you get wine."

"So, Ariel," Finn said, "how can you be a dowser when you get out of school? I thought you were going to be a priestess. Won't Inanna be mad?"

"Finn, Finn, Finn. Always hiding behind that sarcastic wit of yours." She reached across the table and clasped his face between her hands. "Inside there is a joyful little boy, just waiting to get out. Set your joy free, Finn. Set it free."

"You're getting syrup on my cheeks," Finn said.

I laughed, spurting orange juice back into my glass.

"She laughed," Ariel said to Finn.

"So she did," Finn said.

Ariel cast her eyes to the ceiling. "Oh, heavenly day."

CHAPTER 16

AT ENTRÉES ON TRAYS THAT EVENING, Ariel and I had fun. Nothing phenomenal, nothing earth-shattering, but fun. This time Ariel got the privilege of delivering Mrs. Gladstone's pasta with asparagus tips, and when she got back to her car, she went on about what a truly troubled woman Mrs. Gladstone was. It was the first time I'd heard her be the slightest bit grouchy, and I enjoyed it.

"Did she mention her soon-to-be-fragrant urine?" I asked, holding down the talk button on the walkie-talkie.

"She nibbled on the asparagus *while I was there*. She was practically orgasmic."

I laughed, then pulled into the Fish Market's parking lot. "Gotta run," I said. "Over and out."

At 9:15, we met at Darlin's to turn in our money and equipment. Ariel brought tempura from Ichiban's, so I hung out with Darlin and her for a while instead of heading straight home.

"So-o-o?" Ariel said from her perch on the kitchen counter. "Are we Supper Clubbing it again this week? They're going to Portofino. Best pesto in town."

"Ariel," I said. I glanced at Darlin, expecting her to blush and say that maybe she'd go again, but only if I came, too. Which maybe I would, if they begged.

But Darlin smiled and dipped a chunk of fried zucchini into the soy sauce. Her red fingernails looked like pieces of candy. "Oh, girls," she said, "I don't think so."

"Darlin, why not?" Ariel said. "Didn't you have a good time? And what about Phil? It was so obvious he liked you. I thought you liked him, too."

"I liked him just fine," Darlin said. "As a matter of fact, I spoke with him just last night."

"*You did*? Did he ask you out? Are you going?"

"He asked, but I declined."

"But . . ." Ariel shook her head. "You don't have to go out with Phil if you don't want to, but that doesn't mean you have to quit the whole group. Lissa and I will go with you if you don't want to go alone. Right, Lissa?"

"She said she doesn't want to," I said.

Darlin patted Ariel's leg. "Baby, I'm glad you encouraged me to go last Wednesday. It was a good thing. But I watched Phil and the others, and you know what I realized? I'm not like them."

My face got hot. Darlin had found the others wanting, just as I did, but hearing it said out loud made me feel bad.

"With Burl, it was all about how I could please him," Darlin went on. "All those plates of hors d'oeuvres? And heavens, *Antiques Roadshow* week after week? Those folks in the

Supper Club, now, they know how to go about making themselves happy. I've got to learn that all over again."

I stopped chewing. She didn't look down on them. That wasn't it at all.

"I still don't understand why you have to quit the group," Ariel said. "Why can't you hang out with them *while* you figure out how to make yourself happy?"

Darlin laughed. "Gracious, Ariel. Give me time. Right now I need to do some good old-fashioned soul-searching, and believe me, that's a big enough task for anyone."

I looked at Darlin, her face pale with powder, her lips full and pink. She met my gaze, and it was as if she could tell what I was thinking. That maybe *I* needed to do some soul-searching, too. Something passed between us, and she reached over and squeezed my hand.

Later, as Ariel and I walked to our cars, Ariel said she didn't want to go home yet. She was going to Java Jive's for a latte—did I want to come?

The night air smelled like rain, and it was just chilly enough to need a jacket. I wrapped my arms around my ribs and convinced myself that despite Darlin's good example, searching my soul wasn't something I had to do this very second.

"Sure," I said.

It was drizzling by the time we got there, and Ariel and I dashed from the parking lot to the shelter of the coffeehouse. Inside, Ariel shook out her hair. "Brr," she said. "I hate getting water down my collar. Feels like icicles."

"What I hate is water inside my shoes," I said. "How clammy your socks get."

"Uh-huh. I love it when it rains in the summer, but when it's cold out, it just makes everything icky." She weaved through the eating area, which was full despite the late hour. "Hey, today was a good day, wasn't it? Even though Darlin's giving up on the Supper Club."

"She's not giving up," I said defensively. "She's just . . . doing things her own way."

Ariel glanced at me. "I guess," she said. "All I meant was that I had fun with her tonight. I wish we could hang out more."

I felt embarrassed, as if I'd overreacted. "Well, we still can," I said. "It just won't be with the Supper Club."

"Yeah, maybe." She perked back up. "And this morning at IHOP—that was awesome. Finn's great, don't you think?"

"Yeah, he's a nice guy."

"And isn't he *cute*? In a James Dean kind of way, all tough edges and sensual mouth. God, he would hate it if he knew we were talking about him!"

We found an empty table by the window and shrugged off our wet jackets.

"I take it y'all are going out?" I asked.

"Who, me and Finn? Nah, we're just friends. Anyway, he likes brunettes, remember?"

It took me a second, and then blood rushed to my cheeks. I could feel it. When I finally spoke, it was to say the only thing I could think of. "So, uh, what happened to his hand, anyway?"

Her eyes narrowed. "Why? Does it bother you?"

"No, I . . ."

"Because I don't even notice it anymore. It's not that big of a deal."

"No, I know. I was . . . I was just curious."

Her mouth stayed tight, but by the time the server had taken our orders, she appeared to have let it go. Only now, neither one of us could think of anything to say. It was easier over the walkie-talkies.

She drummed her fingers on the table.

I fiddled with the saltshaker.

"Oh, man, I had this crazy dream last night," she said at last. "Want to hear it?"

My heart sank. Dreams? Again?

"Never mind," she said, scanning my face.

"No, it's okay. Let's hear it."

She looked at me, gnawing on her thumbnail. She wiped her thumb on her sleeve and dropped her hand to her lap. "Well . . . I dreamed I was upside down, hanging off the bottom of the planet. There was no one else around, just me, dangling off this giant blue and green globe." She kind of laughed. "Weird, huh?"

The server arrived with our drinks, and I watched as Ariel dumped sugar into her mocha latte, stirred it in, and licked a glob of whipped cream from the spoon.

"So what do you think it means?" I asked.

"God, don't ask me." Again, she laughed. "That I'm all alone in my own little world?"

My face must have registered how awkward I felt, because she gave me a funny look and said, "I was *joking*." She grabbed a third pack of sugar. "Although my mom would beg to disagree."

"Why?"

"I don't know. She hates my hair. She hates my nose ring. She thinks I look like a tramp. Or an alien, depending on her mood. Last night it was a tramp, just because I was wearing this totally normal black camisole. I mean, it wasn't trashy or anything. 'Don't you even want to fit in?' she kept saying."

I cupped my hands around my coffee. She was telling me too much.

"It used to really bug me when she'd yell at me," Ariel said. "I'd think maybe there *was* something wrong with me, you know?"

"But . . . not anymore?"

"Nope. I could care less if I fit in, because—aha! *Aha!* Because I am on the earth, but not of the earth! That's what my dream meant!" She smacked the table. "Shit. Am I well-adjusted or what?"

I gave her a weak smile. I thought of her expression when she called me over to sit with her last week in the cafeteria. The only other person at her table was Finn, and it was a big table.

"God, dreams are cool, aren't they?" Ariel said. She spooned up a sip of her drink. "Wouldn't it be amazing if you could dream things on purpose? Whatever you wanted, just set your mind to it and make it happen?"

My stomach got all fluttery. I opened my mouth, then closed it. Then I thought about how much Ariel had shared, and how little I'd given in return. "You mean . . . like lucid dreaming?"

"What's lucid dreaming?"

The fluttery feeling grew stronger. "It's what my book is about. The one you saw."

114

Ariel drew her eyebrows together.

"On my dashboard? That night at Darlin's? The guy who wrote it taught himself how to control his dreams."

Ariel put down her spoon. "Holy cats. Does he tell how? Have you done it?"

"Well, there are a lot of different methods," I said. I fingered the edge of the table. "I've, um . . . I've tried a couple of them, just for the hell of it, but nothing's really happened."

She looked so fascinated that I almost wanted to tell her the truth: that something *had* happened, a huge something. But I didn't.

"Tell me what you're supposed to do," Ariel said. "I read this one book where this guy would look at his palm during his dreams, and that would make him realize he was dreaming. I've tried, but I can never remember to look at my hand."

"Yeah, a lot of the methods have to do with remembering to do something when you're asleep," I said. "Like, if you see any writing, you're supposed to make yourself look at it more than once."

"Why?"

"Because it'll probably be different the second time around. Instead of saying 'mouse,' it'll say 'elephant,' or whatever. And then you're supposed to think, 'Wait a minute— that can't be right.' And hopefully you'll realize it *isn't* right, and you'll figure out you're dreaming."

"Look for writing," Ariel said, as if ticking off an item on a list.

"Or you can look at a watch. Or a clock. Same concept."

"Isn't it interesting how dreams shift around like that? How things change before you know it, and nothing's what you think it is?"

I gazed at the window, at the glaze of rain on the glass. Then I turned back to Ariel. I made myself meet her eyes. "Another way is to jump up, or fall, or fling yourself backward—anything that gets you into the air."

"What does that do?" Ariel asked.

I shrugged. "If you jump up, you might end up flying instead of thunking back down. Same with the others. And that would tell you it was a dream." I watched her face, seeing too much excitement and not enough wariness. "But none of these are guaranteed, you know. You've got to want it to happen, and you've got to keep working at it. It really has to matter to you."

Ariel leaned forward. "Let's do it. You want to? We can both try to have a lucid dream, and then we can report back on our progress. Like exercise buddies. Or study buddies. Only we'll be dream buddies instead."

My body tightened. Why had I told her all this? What had I been thinking?

The moment stretched out, and I knew I had to give her an answer. Already her smile was changing. I'd hurt her feelings too many times to do it again.

"Sure," I said heavily.

Her smile came back full force. "Fabulous," she said. "This is going to be so cool!"

Afterward, as we paid our tab at the front of the coffeehouse, Ariel brought our conversation back to Finn. "He would love talking about this stuff," she told me. "Lucid dreaming, I mean. Even if he sat there smirking, I know he'd get a kick out of it."

"Maybe," I said. I did not want her talking about it with Finn.

"I know he seems all superior and condescending, but really he's not. Once you get to know him, I mean."

I pocketed my change and headed for the door.

"So if he asked you out, would you go?" she asked.

My head snapped around. "What?"

"If Finn asked you out, would you go?"

"I—I—"

She looked a little pissed, as if it were her I'd rejected. "I guess that's a 'no,' huh?"

"No," I said. "I just . . ."

Ariel folded her arms over her chest. "He's a great guy, Lissa."

"I know."

"So why don't you want to go out with him? Is it his hand?"

"*No!*"

"Relax!" Ariel said. Her expression softened. "I'm kidding. I know you're not like that."

I stood there.

"You're just shy," she said. "But think about it, okay?"

Outside, a car cruised by, spraying water from under its wheels. Ariel glanced out the window and grimaced. "Lovely," she said. "We're going to get soaked." She pulled her jacket tighter around her. "Ready?"

I nodded, and she pushed open the heavy glass door.

CHAPTER 17

SUNDAY NIGHT, JERRY INVITED Sophie over for dinner. This in itself was amazing, and what was equally amazing was the fact that Jerry planned to cook the entire meal by himself. Not tacos, not hamburgers, not grilled-cheese sandwiches, but spinach lasagna, a dish Beth and I had never even had. Jerry was a big meat eater—his favorite snack was a Slim Jim and a box of saltines—which meant that Beth and I, by virtue of living with him, were pretty big meat eaters, too. Sophie was a vegetarian.

"Do you have a recipe?" I said. "Tell me you have a recipe."

"No recipe," Jerry said over his shoulder. He was down on his hands and knees, digging through one of the lower cabinets. "I'll make it up as I go along."

Beth and I shared a look. Once he made grilled-cheese sandwiches with a layer of clams; another time he substituted venison for ground beef on a Chef Boyardee pizza. He was also a big fan of canned corn. Pick a dish, any dish at all, and at the drop of a hat he'd throw in a can of corn. Not as a side dish, but as part of the main dish itself.

"You're not going to put corn in it, are you?" Beth asked.

"Aha! Found it!" He backed out of the cabinet and stood up with a nine-by-eleven-inch glass pan. "I thought I'd make a salad, too. Do we have any mandarin oranges?"

"Mandarin oranges?" I repeated. "Sure. I try to keep a few cans around for emergencies."

He eyeballed me, then set the pan on the counter and fished a twenty-dollar bill from his wallet. "Here. Run to the A & P for me, will you? I need mandarin oranges, lettuce, tomato paste—hold on, I better write this down." He scribbled a list on the back of a receipt. "Don't take too long. I want the sauce to have time to simmer."

As we climbed into the truck, Beth said, "Who was that in our kitchen, and what happened to the real Jerry?"

I smiled. "He's just nervous. This is a big deal for him."

"A huge deal. He's, like, actually excited. Do you think he'll kiss her?"

"Not during dinner, I hope." I turned on the engine and pulled out of the driveway.

"*Afterward*, dummy. When he walks her to her door. That's when the man makes his move."

"Says who?"

"Says Vanessa. And the woman pretends she doesn't want him to, but really she does."

"And then they have a mad, passionate affair on the front steps, and the neighbors come out and cheer."

"Lissa," Beth said.

"Beth."

She clamped her lips together.

"Vanessa is not the queen of the world," I told her. "You can't believe everything she tells you."

"Duh."

We pulled up to a stoplight. "Hey. Tonight's going to be fun, okay?"

"Lissa," she said.

"What?"

"The light's green. Drive."

Sophie showed up at seven o'clock sharp, wearing a fuzzy pink sweater and a denim skirt. She looked different than she looked at the nursery, more made-up, and her smile was friendly but slightly tense. It was a nervousness I recognized, because I always felt stiff when I made an effort to look nice. But I wouldn't have expected it from Sophie.

She handed me a blue plastic plate stacked with brownies. "Double-chocolate," she told us.

"Great," I said. "Thanks." I took them into the kitchen, along with the ice cream she'd brought to go on top. When I returned, Jerry and Sophie were standing awkwardly in the hallway, neither of them saying a word. Beth looked at me with urgent eyes. Do *something*, her expression said.

"Should we move into the den?" I asked. It was the most hostess-y thing I could think of.

Jerry let his breath out in a whoosh. "Sure. Good idea."

"Lead the way," Sophie said.

"So, Sophie," I said once we were seated. "What's new with you?"

"Oh, nothing." She touched her hair, which clung in tight curls to her head. "I got my hair cut this afternoon. That's always a treat."

I couldn't relate, but I nodded. "It looks good."

"Thanks."

We went through another round of smiling and nodding. Why didn't Jerry say anything? And why didn't *Sophie* say anything, for God's sake?

"You like working at the nursery?" I asked.

"I do," she said. "I absolutely love it." Her fingers strayed again to her hair before she caught herself and clasped her hands in her lap.

Jerry slapped his palms against his knees. "Let's eat," he said.

We stood up and filed into the kitchen, where we each grabbed a plate and served ourselves from the buffet Jerry had set up.

"Everything smells heavenly," Sophie said once we were seated around the table. She tasted the lasagna. "Mmm. Delicious."

I took a bite and tried to hide my surprise. "Yeah, Jerry, it's great."

Jerry's neck turned red. "The first one I made was god-awful. I had to dump it in the compost and start over."

And then there was another long gap when no one said a word. Sophie took another bite of lasagna, chewed, and then stopped. But she didn't swallow. I think she was worried about being too loud.

"How's Q.T.?" Beth asked.

"Q.T.?" Sophie said. "My sweet little cat?" She chewed again and now she went ahead and swallowed. "He is the most darling thing, but gracious, he is a handful." Her face lit up as she went into a litter box–training story, and I thought, *Beth has nailed it. Beth has saved the day.*

"Tell about the time he got trapped in the freezer," Jerry said.

"Jerry, no," Sophie said.

"Q.T. got trapped in the freezer?" Beth said.

"Tell her," Jerry said.

Beth put down her fork. "Tell me!"

"Oh, all right." Sophie pursed her lips like she was embarrassed, then began. "Well, Beth, I always like to get up in the morning and go for a walk before driving to work. My morning constitutional. And I like to take a chilled water bottle along with me. So first thing when I get up, I go down to the kitchen, fill my water bottle and pop it into the freezer. That way it's got time to get cold while I'm putting on my sweats and sneakers." She broke off and shook her head. "Jerry, why in the world am I telling this story?"

"You have to," Beth said. "You started it, so you have to finish it."

Jerry caught my eye and grinned.

"All right. Just let me have a little bite to eat to keep up my strength." She took a bite of lasagna and washed it down with her iced tea. "Now where was I?"

"You put your water bottle in the freezer," Beth prompted.

"That's right. And as a rule I am very careful *not* to let Q.T. climb in when I go to get my water bottle out, because strange as it sounds, Q.T. just loves climbing into that freezer. I think because of the frozen fish."

"I thought you were a vegetarian," I said.

"Everything but fish. I can't give up fish. Anyway, on this particular morning—oh, it was three weeks ago, I suppose—Q.T. must have been especially quick, or I must have been especially sleepy, because he hopped into that freezer and I had no idea. I went for my walk like usual, and when I returned—"

"You shut Q.T. in the freezer?" Beth cried.

"I didn't see him!"

"Poor Q.T.!"

"When I finally found him, he was as stiff as a board. His fur was frozen in little spikes, and there was frost on his whiskers. I thought for sure he was dead, but you never know. You hear of people falling through icy lakes, then being resuscitated hours later. Sometimes there's brain damage, but sometimes they're just fine."

I nodded that way you do when you think someone's slightly crazy. Jerry, at the head of the table, smiled and shook his head. He seemed happy in a way I'd never seen before.

"So what did you do?" Beth said. "I mean, he's still alive, isn't he?"

Sophie plucked a slice of orange from her salad. "Well, I called the vet. His name is Dr. Petty—isn't that a hoot? I always said, that is the perfect name for a veterinarian. And he got on the line and said, 'Sophie, do you have a power mower?' At first I had no idea what he was talking about, but then I figured out that he meant did I have a lawn mower. And yes, I did, so I told him so. 'Go out to your garage and siphon some gasoline from the tank,' he said. 'Not a lot, just a thimbleful. Then pry open Q.T.'s jaws and pour the gas down his throat.'"

"Nuh-uh," Beth said.

"That's exactly what I thought, too," Sophie said. "But I figured he was the doctor, and so I did what he said. I pried open Q.T.'s tiny jaws and poured in a drop of gas, and then I got back on the phone and said, 'Okay, Dr. Petty, I did what you said but nothing's happening.' And he said that was his best advice and to give it a minute, but if nothing happened soon, then that was that and he was real sorry. And then he had to get off because he had another patient, a dog with a chicken-soup can stuck in its throat."

It occurred to me that there was really no reason for me to have worried that no one would have anything to say. Give her an opening and Sophie had enough to say for all of us.

"So what happened?" Beth demanded. Her lasagna had gone untouched for five minutes.

"At first, nothing," Sophie said. "I had just about figured him for a goner when his little left paw gave a twitch, like this." She flopped her hand at the wrist. "And then his whole body gave a shake, and then another, until he was writhing around like he was possessed by a demon." Again she demonstrated, shuddering and letting her tongue loll from side to side.

She stilled her body and leaned forward. "And I said, 'Yes, Q.T., you're my fighter, my brave angel boy,' and all of a sudden he was up and gone, like a bolt of lightning had struck him on the tail! Racing through the kitchen, through the den, trying to climb the curtains and making it halfway up before he fell, then back again into the kitchen where he leaped up on the table and skidded all the way from one end to the other and then fell splat onto the floor—"she smacked her hands together"—and just lay there! Didn't move a muscle!"

She stared at us, wide-eyed, and we stared back. Beth's jaw hung open. And then Sophie relaxed her features and speared a piece of lettuce. "This salad is delicious, Jerry. I would truly like the recipe."

Beth banged the table with her palm. *"So what happened?!* Did he . . . did he die?"

"Die? Why no, honey. He just ran out of gas!" She let out a peal of laughter.

Jerry rubbed Beth's head with his knuckles. "She got me the first time, too."

"You mean it didn't happen? None of it?" Beth looked at me indignantly, and I smiled and lifted my shoulders. I'd fallen for it, too, but I didn't want to say so out loud.

"Poor Q.T.," Jerry said, "ran out of gas."

A snicker escaped, and Beth gave in. "Ha. I'm going to tell that story to Vanessa and Nikki, but I'll say it was a guinea pig, because Nikki has a guinea pig named Noel. Do you think it would work with a guinea pig?"

"I don't see why not," Sophie answered.

The phone rang and Beth leaped to get it. "Maybe that's Nikki now." She picked up the receiver. "Hello?"

Jerry and Sophie turned back to their dinner. "You're good with kids," he said, stabbing his last bite of lasagna.

"Back in Alabama, I spent every weekend with my nieces and nephews," she said. "I miss them."

Beth appeared at my side. Her eyes were big. "Lissa, phone."

I stood up and strode across the kitchen. "Hello?"

"Lissa. Hi."

My legs went hollow.

"Are you there?"

"Hold on." I put the receiver on the counter. "Beth, hang up for me. I'm going upstairs."

Her chair scraped the floor.

"Okay, I got it," I called from my room. I waited until Beth hung up, then took my hand off the mouthpiece. "Hi, Kate."

C H A P T E R

18

"WHAT'S UP?" KATE SAID. "Am I interrupting something?
I heard people talking."

"We were eating dinner. Jerry kind of has a date over—this
woman, Sophie, that he knows from work."

"*Jerry* has a *date*? Yikes."

"I know. Big step, huh?"

"Extremely," Kate said.

"At first I thought she was a goof—and she is—but I like
her anyway." I lowered my voice. "She has a cat named Q.T."

"Q.T.?"

"As in the initials. As in, 'He sure is a cutie pie, my Q.T.'"

Kate snorted. "Oh no."

"Oh yes."

"Lord. Well, maybe I should call back later, let you finish
eating."

"That's okay. I was pretty much done anyway."

There was a pause. Talking about Jerry had been easy, and for a second we'd been able to pretend things were normal between us.

"So, why didn't you call me?" Kate asked. "I told you to call me, but you never did."

I sat down on the edge of my bed. "I don't know. I was busy."

"You were busy?"

Another pause.

"Look," Kate said, "this is dumb. We haven't had a fight like this since . . ." She struggled to come up with other examples. "This is really dumb," she said again.

"I agree."

"So can't we *stop*? I mean, God, Lissa, I miss you. I miss talking to you."

My hand, which had been twisting the cord, grew still. "Me, too."

"Then are we friends again? Can we stop acting so retarded around each other?"

I saw her in my mind, how she'd be lying on the floor with her legs crossed up on the wall. That was how she always talked on the phone. "I think that would be good," I said.

"Thank God. I thought I was going to die for a while there. No one got my dumb jokes."

"What about Ben?"

"Ben? Lissa, Ben and I broke up. Didn't you know that?"

Something lifted inside of me. "You and Ben broke up?"

"Yeah. Turns out he's an asshole. Go figure."

"What happened?"

"He got drunk at Terri Anderson's party. Started dancing around in this hideous robe he found in her mom's closet."

I smiled.

"And then he ended up in a corner with Alice Spradling. End of story."

"What—they were fooling around?"

"Yep."

I stared at my jeans. The lightness I'd felt was gone. "Funny how that happens, huh? Get drunk, fool around . . . end of story."

"What are you talking about, Lissa?"

I gripped the phone. I couldn't believe I'd said that, and now I didn't know how to take it back. And part of me didn't want to take it back, wanted Kate to hear it and respond and . . . and just *talk* to me about it.

"I thought we decided not to fight anymore," Kate said. Her voice was cool.

"I'm not fighting. I just . . . I think we need to talk."

"About what? There's nothing to talk about."

"Kate, come on." My heart pounded. "That night? At Rob's house?"

There was a long silence.

"We were drunk," Kate finally said.

"You were. I wasn't."

"I know."

I let out a sharp laugh. "So, what? I'm the big lesbian freak and you're just sweet, innocent Kate who got drunk?"

"Lissa—"

"It wasn't like that, Kate."

I could hear her breathing. I knew she was chewing on her cheek, the way she did when she was upset. She said something quick and low, something about Mike Palermo.

"What?" I said.

"Yesterday in French," she said a little louder. Angry, but at least she was talking. "He said he knew this girl, Susie someone. That he saw her at Piedmont Park, that she and this other girl. . . . He called them rug munchers."

My eyebrows pulled together. Rug munchers? Then I got it, and my face burned. "He's an idiot."

"My dad plays golf with his dad."

"So?"

"So . . . I don't know. What if he—"

"Kate, please. This is us, remember?"

"I know. And what happened at . . ." She swallowed. "I'm not saying, you know, that I *blame* you, or that I think it's your fault, but—"

"What?!"

"I'm just saying there's no point in talking about it. Can't we just drop it?"

I fought the pressure rising in my chest. "I don't *want* to drop it!"

"Well, screw you," she said, all tight now and glassy-sharp. Her voice made a hiccup-y sound. "Thanks for being there, Lissa. Thanks a lot." There was a click, and the line went dead.

I couldn't think. My breath came fast and I could hear my pulse in my head. I banged down the phone and stumbled downstairs.

"Lissa?" Jerry called.

The screen door slammed behind me as I ran to my truck. The tires hit the curb hard as I backed out of the driveway, and I swore and shifted into first. Once out of my neighborhood, I headed east on Lindberg, then took Lindberg to I-85. Since it was Sunday, the highway was nearly empty. I merged into the far left lane and drove.

Kate. That night at Rob's house. *I'm not saying that I blame you . . .* God, when *she* was the one who started things. *She* was the one who kissed *me*. Was she in such denial that she didn't even remember?

It was after the guys had started smoking cigars, after Kate had looked at me and made a show of coughing and waving her hand. "Come on," she'd said. "Let's get out of here." She grabbed my hand and pulled me outside, sprinting across the lawn to the gazebo. We dropped to the floor and pressed our backs against the inside wall. From the house, no one could see us.

"Much better," Kate said. "I'm sorry, but there is only so much Aqua Velva I can take in one night. Somebody needs to sit Rob down and explain the concept of moderation, and it's not going to be me."

"Oh, come on," I said. "I bet he'd give you a cigar."

Kate grimaced. "Do they seriously not know how stupid they look? How can that be?"

We ragged on them a little longer, tossing out comments to make each other laugh, and then Kate reached inside her jacket and pulled out a silver flask. "Compliments of Travis Wyrick," she said.

I raised my eyebrows. "Oh yeah?"

"He was passed out in the kitchen, and Gretchen Ragsdale was patting his hand and singing a lullaby. I figured I was doing him a favor."

"Uh-huh. What's in it?"

She unscrewed the lid and sniffed. "Gin? Vodka?" She tipped the flask into her mouth. "Vodka. Want some?"

I took a sip and made a face.

"Yeah. We need orange juice or something." She took

another swallow. "So. Lissa. Summer's almost over."

"Mm-hmm."

"I don't want it to be. I want things to go on like this forever."

I'd spent almost every day at her neighborhood pool, every night at her house. "Me, too."

Crickets chirped in Rob's yard. A breeze blew through the gazebo, stirring Kate's hair.

"You excited about school?" she asked.

"Not really. But I'm not dreading it."

She lifted the flask one last time, then screwed on the top and put it away. "I am. I don't want to deal with everybody. I don't want to deal with who's seeing who and who's wearing what and all that crap. I just want to hang out with you and do nothing, like we always do."

"Thanks a lot."

"No, I mean it in a good way. You're my best friend, Lissa. You're wonderful. Everyone else makes me feel like I'm so—I don't know. Not me." She leaned against me and closed her eyes. "Whoa. I'm getting woozy. Cheap date, huh?"

Her head was heavy on my shoulder, and I could smell the vanilla she'd dabbed behind each ear. She fingered the bottom of my T-shirt. "Hey," she said, "remember when we talked about what it would be like to kiss another girl? What it would feel like?"

"Yeah?"

"Want to try? You know, just as an experiment?"

I kind of laughed. "Oh, like for the good of humankind? 'Girl Kisses Girl and Saves the—'"

She lifted her head. Her lips grazed mine.

"Huh," I joked. "You taste like vodka." I pressed my palm against my leg.

"You taste like you." She kissed me again, and my lips parted against hers. My heart whammed beneath my ribs.

Kate moved so that she was lying on the floor. She slipped her hand beneath my shirt, touched the small of my back, and I lowered myself so that I was lying beside her, our bodies parallel. Her thighs, her hips, her breasts pressed against me. Her lips on mine.

Heat flooded through me. I had tried to block that night from my mind for so long that now, alone on the highway, I felt like I was hyperventilating. I flicked on my blinker and got off at the next exit, then pulled into a Stuckey's parking lot and cut the engine. I tried to steady my breathing.

We didn't hear Rob and Ben until they were halfway across the yard, only feet from the gazebo. Kate jerked herself up, ran her fingers through her hair.

"Kate," I said.

She shot me a panicked glance, then made a point of looking at the floor, at her hands, anywhere but at me. She grabbed the flask and quickly unscrewed it so it would look like we'd just been out there drinking. "Get up. Hurry!"

I fumbled with my bra, tugged down my shirt. By the time Rob stepped inside, Kate was on her feet, grinning and not paying attention to me at all.

We never talked about it, not until tonight. Kate went back to the house with Ben and had three more beers before throwing herself all over him. I watched from the doorway, then walked out the front door and didn't look back. Monday, the first day of school, Kate ignored me and I ignored her. But no matter how much we denied it, we both knew that what happened was more than an experiment or a drunken mistake. Otherwise, why would we care? Why wouldn't we just laugh about it and move on?

What Kate and I felt was real, and screw her for pretending it wasn't. And screw me, too. I was sick of running away.

CHAPTER 19

THAT NIGHT I HAD THE DREAM AGAIN, the one about walking off with a stranger. Only this time there was no stranger, and no Cookie Churchill either. This time I'd been walking across the parking lot, and someone had whistled at me, one of those wolf whistles, like, *Over here, hot mama.* I turned at the sound and saw Ben Porter and Rob Lynch leaning against a car and looking cocky as hell. They laughed and slapped each other a high five, and I'd jerked awake. And now, sitting up in my bed, my heart was still pounding. My scalp prickled, and even though it was four in the morning and I was alone in my room, I couldn't shake the feeling that I was being watched.

I got a drink of water from the bathroom, then went downstairs and switched on the TV. There was no point in going back to bed. I pushed the up arrow on the remote and skimmed through the channels. On TNT, before-and-after pictures of a girl with acne flashed on the screen. The shot changed to show the same girl sitting with a dark-haired boy, laughing and holding hands, and the name of a product appeared in bold letters. "Miracle Salve—Because Who Doesn't Need a Miracle?"

I heard the floor creak, and I glanced over my shoulder to see Jerry standing in the doorway.

"Couldn't sleep?" he said. His hair was sticking up funny, and he was wearing his ratty blue sweats.

"Was I too loud? Sorry." I muted the TV.

"Leave it on if you want. Doesn't bother me." He came around the sofa and dropped down beside me. He watched as the infomercial began again, then said, "Your mom and I used to watch TV together, back when your dad was putting in such long hours at his firm. I'd come over to help with you kids, and then your mom and I would find some old movie and sit up watching it until Dan got home."

He'd told me that before, but I didn't mind hearing it again.

"You have her coloring," he said. "You look more and more like her every day."

"I don't think so," I said. Mom had been beautiful, with thick brown hair and dark eyes. She'd probably never had a zit in her life.

Jerry spread his hands on his legs. He drummed his fingers, then held them still. "You doing okay, Lissa?"

Blue light flickered on the sofa. On me, curled up with my knees drawn to my chest. "I'm fine," I said. "I drank too much Coke before I went to bed, that's all."

He looked at me. "You left the house in an awful hurry."

I didn't respond.

"I was worried. Sophie and I, we both were."

For some reason that made my muscles tighten. What right did Sophie have to worry?

Jerry cleared his throat. "Anyway, if there's anything I can do, anything you want to talk about . . ."

"There's not," I said. "Really." I forced a smile. "So how *is* Sophie? Seems like things are going well with you two."

His shoulders relaxed. "We have a good time together," he said.

"Great," I said. I hoped I sounded more sincere than I felt, because deep down I *did* want Jerry to be happy. Right now, though, I figured that if I was miserable, everyone else should be, too. Plus, what would it mean if Jerry and Sophie really ended up liking each other? Marrying each other, even?

Jerry settled into the sofa. "It's funny, isn't it? I always figured I'd be one of those guys who ends up alone. Or that I'd have to settle for someone who was just as lonely, and that would be the only reason we got together. But with Sophie . . ."

It was strange, hearing him tell me this. I kept my eyes on the TV.

"Well, we'll see," he finally said. He stood up. "Get some sleep if you can, okay?"

"Yeah. 'Night, Jerry."

"Good night."

After he left, I turned off the TV and leaned back against the couch. Jerry did his best, I knew that, but sometimes it wasn't enough. Sometimes he felt more like a roommate than anything else. Usually that was okay, but tonight it added to my depression.

Guilt washed over me. Jerry had come downstairs to check on me, after all. I could have opened up to him, but I didn't. What more did I want?

My mind flashed to my parents. To Mom. When I was eight, two months before she and Dad died, my elementary school had a medieval parade. Most of the girls dressed up as ladies of the court, wearing tall cone-shaped hats made out of construction paper, but I had decided to go as a knight. I remembered standing in my third-grade classroom, fighting back tears because I couldn't get my costume to work, and looking up to see Mom being led in by one of the teachers. "Oh, Lissa," she said, fingering the pieces of cardboard I'd covered with aluminum foil. She helped tie the pieces to my body, then made me join the parade, even though I no longer wanted to.

At the end of the day, prizes were given for the best costumes. My name was called for "Most Creative," but I pressed close against Mom's leg and refused to walk to the front of the room. I thought the judges felt sorry for me. I didn't want everyone looking at me.

"Go on," Mom said, kissing the top of my head. Afterward, she told me my costume was fine, that I needed to have more faith in myself. "You were faced with a hard situation, and you handled it. I'm proud of you."

That was one of the last memories I had of her.

I stretched my leg so that my foot reached the coffee table, my toes curling against its edge. If Mom were still alive, would I talk to her about this stuff with Kate? Probably not, just as I didn't tell Jerry. Still. Like a trace of perfume, I had a feeling that if I did, she would have understood.

CHAPTER 20

"YIKES," ARIEL SAID, "what happened to you?"

I yanked my biology book from my locker.

"You look exhausted," she continued.

"I didn't get much sleep," I said.

"Why not?"

"I don't know. I just didn't." I closed my locker and strode down the hall.

"Wait!" she cried. She jogged to catch up. "What are you doing after school today?"

I glanced at her, and for the first time I noticed her hair, which was no longer burgundy. Now it was a pale orange, and so short that it stuck up in little tufts all over her head. She looked like a baby chick.

"Nice hair," I said.

Her hand flew to the top of her head. "Really? You like it?"

"Yeah. It looks good."

"My mom hates it—big surprise. My dad didn't even notice."

"He had to have noticed. He probably just didn't know what to say. Jerry pulls that kind of stuff all the time."

She shook her head. "Nope. He didn't notice."

We entered the stairwell and navigated our way through the crowd. It was too noisy to talk, so Ariel waited until we reached the second floor before asking, "What about this afternoon? Are you busy?"

"All I want to do is go home and take a nap."

"Take a nap later. Come to Memorial Park and hang out with me and Finn."

"Why?"

"What do you mean, why? Because it'll be fun. Because it's a nice day."

The bell rang and the hall emptied out. "I don't know," I said, stopping outside the biology room.

"Meet us at Memorial, over by the swing set. Around three o'clock."

"Maybe."

Ms. Horowitz reached to close the door, and I ducked inside.

By the end of sixth period I was a zombie. My head throbbed if I moved too suddenly, and my eyes burned in a dry, gritty way as if my eyelids were coated with sand. On top of that I felt incredibly grubby, because at around 6:00 A.M. I'd gotten sucked into an old *Highway to Heaven* episode about a lost dog, and I'd run out of time to shower. As far as I was concerned, the whole day was a write-off, and all I wanted to do was go home and crash. Maybe watch a little TV. Hah.

I slumped in front my locker, trying to decide which books

to bring home, when out of the corner of my eye I glimpsed long blond hair. My breath caught in my throat.

"Lissa," Kate said.

I grabbed the book on top of the stack and shoved it into my backpack.

"Lissa, I'm sorry about last night. I was a huge jerk."

"Yeah, you were."

She gnawed on her thumbnail, but she didn't turn away.

"Well, I'm sorry, too," I said. I shut my locker. "But not for what you think."

Her eyes flicked to the end of the hall, then back to me. "I know. Me, too. And I know we didn't mean anything by it, but . . ." Her voice practically disappeared. "Come on. It's just not normal."

My heart lurched. "What's not normal?"

She didn't answer.

"*Me?* You think *I'm* not normal?" I tried to push past her, but she grabbed my arm.

"You know that's not what I mean. God!" Her fingers tightened on my skin, and then she let go, wrapping her arms around her ribs.

"What? Can't bear to touch me?"

"Stop it. Stop being this way."

We stared at each other.

"I'm trying to apologize," she said. Her voice trembled. "Can't we stop obsessing about this and just be friends again? Please?"

I looked at her. Her hair, so different from Ariel's, hung loose around her face, and her eyebrows were drawn together in an unhappy line. She wore silver earrings shaped like dolphins, the earrings I'd given her on her fifteenth birthday. Yearning swept over me, a huge rush of desire for things to go back to how they were.

I let go. So hard until I did it, and then so easy once it was done. "That would be good," I said.

Kate smiled. She gave me a hug—a quick one, not too close—then stepped back, glancing at her watch. "Ah, shit. Lissa, I've got to run. I've got gymnastics practice, which normally I could skip, except—"

"It's okay," I said. "It's fine."

"Yeah. Well . . ."

"Really. It's no big deal."

"I'll call you, all right?"

"Sure. Whatever." I watched her walk down the hall. She stopped at the door, waved, then disappeared around the side of the building.

I closed my eyes. What had I just done? What happened to old-fashioned soul-searching, to my decision to stop pretending? Because I knew that Kate, when she asked if we could be friends, meant only on her terms.

It was just that it felt so good to talk to her, to be near her. To have her look at me and smile.

As for the rest—I didn't want to think about it.

I decided to go to the park.

"Lissa!" Ariel called. She and Finn leaned against a huge oak. Next to them sat a six-pack of Rolling Rock.

"Want one?" Ariel said. She offered me a bottle, shielding her eyes from the sun.

I took it and dropped down beside them. "You have a bottle opener?"

"Twist off," Finn said. He took my bottle and clamped it between his elbow and his side, using his good hand to twist off the cap. "Here you go."

"Thanks," I said. I didn't even know why I'd taken it. I wasn't much of a drinker. But I tilted the bottle and gulped down several swallows.

Ariel stretched out her legs and put her feet in my lap. "Check out these babies," she said, wiggling her shoes. "Aren't they awesome? I got them at Abba-Dabba's."

They were clunky black and white saddle oxfords with thick black laces. "They're nice," I said. "They look . . . durable."

"You bet. They're called Fluevogs. They're made by this little Polish guy off in Poland."

"Go figure," Finn said.

"Check out the soles," she said.

I took another swig of beer, then lifted one of her shoes. On the bottom, carved into the tread, were nine tiny angels. "Huh. That's cool."

"Yep. I have angels on my soul. On my *soul*, get it? And when I walk in the snow, I'll leave baby angel prints everywhere I go."

Finn snorted. "When you walk in the snow, you call me, okay? This is Atlanta, remember?"

"Whatever." She wiggled her foot again, lifting it for me to hold. "Read what's written in the middle."

I held her foot still. "'One hundred percent Natural Hevea-Tree Latex.' What's natural Hevea-tree latex?"

"Not that part. The other part."

I squinted. "'Resists Alkali, Water, Acid, Fatigue, Satan.'" I laughed. "Your shoes resist Satan."

"Why do you think I bought them?"

"Walk with God," Finn said solemnly.

"Walk with God," she repeated. She moved her feet out of my lap. "I got a new nose ring, too." She leaned forward. Embedded above her right nostril was a dark red stone, maybe a garnet.

"She's mad at her parents," Finn said. "She's rebelling. That's why she has the beer—she stole it from her dad."

"Well, you wear it well," I said. "The nose ring, not the beer. Although you drink the beer well. Why are you rebelling?" I finished my beer, then shook my head, which was feeling muzzy. Finn handed me a second Rolling Rock, and I took a long swallow.

"Because they're being assholes," Ariel said. "They want me to be more like my sister."

"Shannon?"

"Uh-huh. She's a cheerleader now. Did I tell you? She puts Vaseline on her teeth so her lips won't get stuck when she smiles."

I laughed. "I hope Beth never does that."

"Is she a cheerleader?" Ariel asked.

"She's ten."

"You never know. They start young, these rah-rah types."

Above us, an airplane flew across the sky.

"I love the trails planes leave," Ariel said. "They look so pretty, like wispy, delicate clouds."

"They're smoke," Finn said. "Exhaust. Pollution."

Ariel swatted him, then scooted down so that her head rested against his thigh. She closed her eyes and said, "I think I'll be a skywriter when I grow up. I'll only write love letters. Love letters in the sky."

"I thought you were going to be a dowser," Finn said.

"Yep. A dowser and a skywriter. What a lovely existence."

Finn looked at me and swiveled his finger by his temple, stopping abruptly when Ariel opened her eyes to see why I was laughing. "Shh," he said in a loud whisper. "We don't want to upset her."

We didn't leave until it got dark, and Finn ended up driving me home. He'd had one beer to my three and, unlike me, he was operating on more than two hours of sleep. At least I assumed he was.

"What about my drunk?" I said. I tried again. "My *truck*?"

"I'll follow behind in your truck," Ariel said, "and then Finn can take me back to my car. How about that?"

"Are you safe to drive?"

She held up two fingers. "Scout's honor. I'm fine."

I stumbled, and Finn put his hand out to steady me.

"Come on," he said, guiding me to his car.

"Wait. I've got to give my keys to Ariel."

She dangled them in front of me. "Already did. Remember?"

I'm not sure what Finn and I talked about on the way home. Pizza, I think, and how good a cheese and pepperoni sounded about then. Mainly I watched Ariel from the rearview window, wincing as she lurched behind us in my truck.

"Looks like she's having some trouble with the stick shift," Finn said.

The truck jolted forward, narrowly missing the curb.

"Uh-huh," I said.

We pulled into my driveway, and Finn cut the engine. He cleared his throat. "So, um, you want to go out for pizza some night?"

I turned to look at him. "Huh?"

"Pizza. Maybe we could go to Fellini's on Saturday, if you want." His hands were in his lap: his right hand covering his too-small left one. I thought of Kate's strong hands, her nails filed short for gymnastics. When she was in junior high, she used to bite them.

"But if you don't want to—"

"No," I said. I banished Kate from my head. "Pizza sounds good. Oh, but I work that night."

"Ariel said she'd cover for you."

"She did?"

"Only if you want her to. I mean, it's up to you." A flush crept up his neck.

"Oh," I said. I felt slow, like my brain wasn't working the way it should. "Well, uh, sure." I opened the door and got out.

"See you later," he called when I was almost to the house.

I looked back. "Right. See you later."

CHAPTER 21

"SO," I SAID THE NEXT DAY at school.

"So," Kate said.

Our eyes met briefly before we both looked away. We'd decided during history to hang out together this afternoon. Only now, standing by our lockers, neither of us knew how to act. It was like we had to get to know each other all over again.

Kate half-laughed and brushed her hand through her hair. "How'd you do on the quiz Mr. Neilson gave us?"

"Okay, I guess. How about you?"

"I bombed it, as usual. I totally forgot who Joseph Smith was."

"The guy who founded Mormonism," I said on reflex. I blushed and tried to think of something else to say.

From the end of the hall came loud male voices, and Kate's eyes flicked toward the sound. Her face paled and she stepped closer to her locker, fiddling with the lock even though she'd already gotten her books.

"What?" I said

"Nothing."

I glanced over my shoulder, and my chest tightened. "Just ignore him. He's an asshole."

They stopped behind us, Ben and Travis Wyrick. "Hi, Kate," Ben said. He nodded at me. "Hi, Lissa. You two going to Travis's this weekend? He's getting a keg."

"Going to be a good time," Travis said.

Kate didn't respond.

I crossed my arms over my chest and said, "I don't think so."

"Kate?" Ben said.

She turned around, but she kept her eyes on the floor. "I can't. I've already got plans."

"Oh," he said. He shifted his weight. "Well, if you change your mind . . ."

"Come on, buddy," Travis said, clapping Ben on the shoulder. "Let's bounce."

I waited until they were out of earshot, then shook my head. "God, talk about ego. He ditches you for Alice Spradling, then has the nerve to act like nothing happened. What a jerk."

"Lissa—"

"What? I mean, if anything you were the one acting guilty, when you have *nothing* to feel guilty about. He's a loser, Kate. Let it go."

Kate fiddled with the strap of her backpack, then folded her arms over her waist and looked past me down the hall. "Let's go to Smoothie King. I'm starving."

Over strawberry smoothies, I told her about my upcoming

date with Finn. I'm not sure why. And for some reason I acted more enthusiastic than I really was, describing our afternoon at the park and how he tried to be so casual when he suggested we go out for pizza. I thought Kate would be excited for me, but she put down her smoothie and gave me an odd smile.

"Finn O'Connor? You're going out with Finn O'Connor?"

"Yep. Saturday night."

"Huh." She crumpled her straw wrapper into a ball. "What about his hand?"

"What about it?"

"Nothing, it's just—" Again, that smile. She flicked the wrapper across the table and said, "That's great, Lissa. That's really great."

I felt off balance, like no decision I made would be right. *You can't have it both ways*, I wanted to tell her. *You can't hate me for kissing you and then act all weird when I go out with someone else.*

But if I said that, Kate would get up and leave. Or she'd close herself off like the other night on the phone.

"Kate, I don't . . ." I spread my hands flat on the table. "It's not like I *like* him or anything."

"Who, Finn?"

I gave her a look.

"Sure you do," she said. "He's a great guy. You'll have a wonderful time."

The bell on the door tinkled, and Kate and I turned our heads. In came a woman wearing a brown coat, nothing special about her, but we both feigned interest as she ordered her smoothie, paid, and left. When she was gone, Kate gazed out the window and I stared at the table. I tried to think of something to talk about. Anything, just so she'd see we could still have fun together.

"Hey," Kate said. She leaned forward over the table. "Did I tell you what happened in English today?"

"What?"

"Well, Mr. Crankshaw was going on and on about something, I don't even know what, and Lissa—" she looked at me and lowered her voice "—I got the hiccups."

For most people, getting the hiccups was no big deal, but for Kate it was an affliction. She couldn't hold them back no matter how hard she tried, and each time she hiccuped it sounded as if a frog were trying to escape from her lungs.

I raised my eyebrows. "So what'd you do?"

"What do you mean, what did I do? I hiccuped. Mr. Crankshaw broke off right in the middle of his lecture and said, 'Young lady, was that a *burp?*'"

I looked at her, how she'd widened her eyes and lifted her hands, and a lump rose in my throat. It wasn't easy for her either, I realized. And she *was* trying.

"I needed you, Lissa. I needed you to give me the cure."

The cure was for Kate to take a deep breath, stare straight at me, and slowly exhale while I counted backward from ten to one. While she exhaled, she was supposed to draw a cow in the air with her finger. Or a poodle. Or a zebra. Once I told her to draw a warthog from hell, and she let out all of her air in a giggling whoosh.

"How'd you finally get rid of them?" I said.

"I ignored them, and finally they went away. It took forever, though."

150

I'd been stirring my smoothie with my straw, but now I stopped. I wondered if she knew what she'd just said. Or was she so good at ignoring things that she even had herself fooled?

She gestured at my Styrofoam cup. "You done with that?"

I wasn't, but I pushed it toward her anyway. It was the least I could do.

CHAPTER

22

ON WEDNESDAY AFTERNOON I took Beth to the High Museum so she could get extra credit in art, and at the last minute I called Kate and asked if she wanted to join us. She said sure, so Beth and I stopped by her house to pick her up.

"There she is," Beth said, spotting Kate jogging down her front steps. "Oh, her coat is so cute. I want a coat like that."

I smiled. I liked Kate's coat, too. It was periwinkle blue with a hood and big buttons up the front, and it reminded me of Paddington Bear.

"Hi," Kate said, opening the door of the truck. Crisp fall air blew in as she climbed onto the seat.

"I love your coat," Beth said. She scooted over to make room. "Where'd you get it?"

"My mom ordered it for me. Somewhere in New York." She pressed her legs together and shut the door.

"Sorry it's so crowded," I said.

"That's okay."

"I could sit in the back," Beth said.

"No," Kate and I said in unison.

"It's dangerous," I added. "You know that."

"Anyway, we want you up here with us." Kate said. She was blushing, but we both ignored it. "You're the whole reason we're going, remember? And I haven't seen you in ages."

Beth beamed and launched into a blow-by-blow of her day, telling us how a boy named Roger lost the fifth-grade gerbil and threw the entire elementary school into a state of chaos.

"I bet it was in somebody's lunch box," Kate said. "Was it in somebody's lunch box?"

"No," Beth said. "How would it get in a lunch box?"

"You never know. Gerbils are tricky. Did it crawl into someone's jacket? Hide in a shoe?"

"No, no, no."

"I know," Kate said. She tickled Beth's side. "It's right here! It's been here all along!"

Beth shrieked and jerked back, and the two of them fell together giggling.

I glanced at them and smiled. This was the way it was supposed to be with me and Kate, even if it took a ten-year-old to smooth things over. I pressed on the accelerator, snapping them, laughing, against the back of the seat.

At the museum, we wandered single file through the post-Impressionist exhibit, listening to the tape-recorded audio tour on individual headsets. All of the paintings were nice, but there was one, a Matisse, that I absolutely loved. It was called *Icarus*, and it showed a man falling through a night sky. The figure of the man was curvy and sprawling, and stars were flung onto the sky so that their points went every which way.

The voice on the audio tour switched to the next painting

before I was ready to move on, so I clicked off the tape and gazed at the figure's outstretched arms. There was a red dot to show where his heart was, the only color on his otherwise solid form.

Kate came and stood beside me. Her earphones hung around her neck. "Wow," she said, studying the Matisse. She took a step closer. "He's the guy who died because he flew too close to the sun, right?"

"Well . . . but look at his heart."

"You mean that one dot?"

"Yeah."

Kate shrugged. "So?"

"It's red, which means he's still alive."

"Until he hits the ground," Kate said. She smacked her hands together. "Splat."

Her comment cut me. I could feel my ears heat up, and I took a step away from her.

For a second Kate looked surprised, and then her mouth drew into a knot. She thought I was being too sensitive, I could tell.

"But he doesn't hit the ground," I said. "In the myth he lands in the sea, remember? Which means there's a chance he survives." I didn't know why I was going on about this, but I couldn't let it go. I wanted Kate to understand.

Kate glanced at me, then back at the Matisse. She didn't respond.

Beth's favorite part of the museum was the children's exhibit on the lower level, and she dragged us there as soon as we finished the tour.

"This is so cool," Kate said when she walked into the first room. Brightly painted metal structures stretched from the floor to the ceiling, an avant-garde jungle gym. "Has this always been here?"

Beth scaled the side, looping her leg over a thick red bar. "Come on! What are you waiting for?"

Kate swung onto one of the bars, then sidestepped toward the middle and climbed higher. I followed, resting midway across to admire Kate's grace as she climbed from bar to bar. Her movements were quick and assured, and she seemed more like herself than she had all day.

"What's the holdup?" she teased when she glanced back to check my progress. The weirdness between us had retreated. "You going to stay there all day?"

"Probably," Beth said. "She's such a slowpoke."

"Excuse me?" I reached for the bar above me and pulled myself up.

After the metal jungle gym came a hall full of twisting mirrors, which we stumbled through with our hands out, grinning at our multiple, clumsy images. Next was an optical illusions room, and following that was a room called "The Magic of Touch," where you could run your fingers over every kind of texture imaginable.

But the last exhibit was the best. I watched Kate's face as we filed in.

"Oh," she said. "Oh, wow." She stared at the far end of the dark room, where heat and motion sensors projected kaleidoscopic images onto the wall-sized screen. She lifted her arm, and an orange figure on the screen lifted her arm as well. She took a step forward, and the figure enlarged. She leaned to the left, and the figure, no longer orange but purple, leaned with her. Colors rippled across the screen like a puddle of rainbows, and in the middle was Kate's outline: slender, pale yellow, her arms moving in a fluid arc above her head.

A turquoise Beth twirled and danced, giggling at her reflected twin, while Kate moved more slowly, swaying back and forth as if she were underwater. I stood still and watched my image shift from one hue to the next. It reminded me of my lucid dreams, that same quality of reality overlaid with fantasy. Enchanted. Surreal.

"Watch this," Beth said. She leaped into the air, and her image splashed across the wall.

"Stunning," Kate said, clapping her hands.

"Now you," Beth said. "Do a cartwheel."

Kate stepped away from us and did a perfect cartwheel. "Your turn," she said to me when she finished.

"It's getting late," I said. "I told Jerry we'd be home by five."

"Oh, come on," she said. She poked me in the ribs until I grinned and twisted away.

"Okay, okay," I said. I raised my hands over my head and shook my hips. "There. Are you happy?"

Beth rolled her eyes. "Kate, do one more thing. Do that flippy-over thing where your hands don't touch the ground. Please?"

"An aerial?" she asked. She lifted her arms, then brought them down quickly and tucked at the waist, flipping her legs over her body. My breath caught in my throat, and I clapped hard to cover what I was feeling.

Beth clapped, too. "Do it again! Do a handspring!"

"No, Beth," I said, "we've really got to go." I started forward, and Kate turned to wait for us. Her profile changed from gold to green, then back to gold.

I fell in beside her, and together we left the exhibit. I was careful not to brush against her, because I was too aware of wanting to. I didn't want her to sense it and pull away. But on the screen, when I glanced back one last time, colors flowed between us as if we were connected.

23

"LISSA, YOU'RE NOT LISTENING," Beth complained on Friday evening.

"Yes, I am," I said. "You were talking about Vanessa, how she's got a new best friend. Mandy something-or-other."

"*Mindy*," Beth said. She draped herself over the back of the sofa, one foot dragging the ground. "Mindy's dad manages the Apparel Mart, and Mindy gets to go whenever she wants and buy jewelry really cheap. Today she and Vanessa wore matching necklaces. Fourteen-carat gold."

"Uh-huh."

"It's terrible! They sit together at lunch and everything!" She shook my shoulder. "Lissa!"

I jerked myself back. "Huh? So they eat together. What's the big deal?"

She slid off the sofa. "You're not paying attention. You don't even care."

"Beth—"

She stomped upstairs and slammed her door.

I closed my eyes. Beth was right; my mind was somewhere else. Today during my free period, I'd gone to the library and accessed the Internet on one of the school computers. My palms had gotten sweaty and my stomach had cramped up, but I'd glanced around to make sure no one was looking and then typed in the word *homosexuality*. Over a thousand pages were found, so I typed in *teenage* to narrow the search. This time there was less information, and most of it was really depressing. Gay teenagers were two to six times more likely to attempt suicide than other teenagers, one study reported, and another said that up to thirty percent of all adolescent suicides were committed by gay teens.

Jesus.

But I also found an on-line magazine called *Prism*, and in it were poems and essays by kids who were gay. Someone named Lucy McDonald had written a poem about loving another girl, and she compared stroking her girlfriend's stomach to running her hands along the inside of a wooden bowl. I read that and I got a breath-catching feeling inside, anxious and full of longing.

When Kate and I were in junior high, there was a game the two of us played where I would close my eyes and hold out my arm, and Kate would walk her fingertips in light, fluttering steps from the inside of my wrist to my elbow. Then we'd switch, and I'd do it to her. The point was for the person with closed eyes to call out "Stop" before the other person got all the way to her elbow, which is harder than it sounds. But really, we did it because we liked the way it felt. It wasn't sexual or anything, no more than tracing letters on each other's backs or fixing each other's hair.

I sank into the sofa and stared at the ceiling. Things were better now that Kate and I were talking again. They were. But in some ways I still missed her so much.

The doorbell rang, rescuing me from my thoughts. Sophie. She was here to take Beth and me shopping—her idea, not ours. I pushed myself up from the sofa. "Beth!" I called. "Sophie's here!"

In the front hall, Jerry opened the door and invited Sophie in. When I joined them, they were standing close together, Sophie's hand on Jerry's arm. She let go when she saw me. "Lissa," she said. "Hi. Ready to go?"

"Sure," I said.

Beth trundled down the stairs.

"Beth, honey, better grab a jacket," Sophie said. "It's chilly. And Jerry, I don't know what you're going to do with yourself all night long, but this is a girls' night out and we're going to have some fun. Isn't that right, girls?"

Beth made a face. She was still mad at me, I could tell, but we were stuck in this together.

"Right," I said. "Let's go."

Beth wanted to check out the jewelry counter at Macy's, so that's where we went first. We each had fifty dollars, given to us by Jerry, and Sophie had thrown in twenty-five apiece on top of that. I told her she didn't need to, but she insisted.

Beth pored over the gold necklaces, tons of them, all different lengths and widths, then pointed to the one she liked the best. The salesclerk separated it from the others and draped it over her fingers. "A hundred sixty-five dollars," she said.

Beth bit her lip.

"You don't have enough money," I said.

"I know."

"Anyway, you shouldn't get one just because Vanessa and Mandy have one."

"*Mindy.*"

"Whatever. I'm not trying to be a jerk, Beth, but you don't even like jewelry."

"How do you know? I *love* jewelry. I've always loved jewelry."

"Beth, honey, how about this?" Sophie said. She held up a delicate gold chain with a pendant shaped like a teddy bear. She took in Beth's expression and wrinkled her brow. "Not your style?"

"Uh, not exactly."

She placed the necklace on the counter. "Well, then, we'll just keep looking. And if I pick out something you don't like, you just tell me. Just say, 'Sophie, that is the *ugliest* necklace I've ever seen.' All right?"

Beth rubbed the toe of her shoe against the floor. "I might not want a necklace after all. I'm not a hundred percent positive one way or the other."

"Should we go look at clothes?" I suggested.

"Yeah. Let's go to The Gap."

Beth found a denim skirt she loved, and Sophie, who turned out to be better at clothes than jewelry, helped her select a couple of shirts to go with it. "Tops," Sophie called them. They were cute.

I grabbed some sweatshirts from the rack, along with some loose-fitting jeans. I'd just about made up my mind when I heard a tap on the dressing-room door.

"Try this," Sophie said, passing a light pink shirt over the top of the door.

"I don't know," I said. I didn't mind the style—it was a V neck with short sleeves—but the fabric was clingy and the cut was snug. Not my kind of thing.

"Just try it," Sophie said.

I sighed and slipped it over my head. I looked at myself in the mirror.

"Well?" Sophie said.

I hesitated, then opened the door.

Sophie's expression went soft. "Oh, honey, that's the one."

I walked to the full-length mirror at the end of the narrow hall and turned sideways. The color went well with my skin, and the way the shirt hugged my body made me look curvy and slender at the same time.

"Wow," Beth said, coming up behind me.

I bought the shirt, as well as a necklace Sophie spotted at one of the jewelry carts in the middle of the mall. No teddy bears this time; this one was an antique-y looking silver chain with tiny blue stones inserted between the links. From the middle dangled a larger stone that rested in the hollow of my throat. It cost $22.99.

"It'll go with your new shirt," Sophie said. "Chokers are perfect for V necks."

While the vendor punched the price into the cash register, Beth fingered a different necklace, one made from a thin leather cord strung with funky purple beads. I watched her for a couple of seconds, then counted the money in my wallet. "Ring that one up, too," I told the guy.

"But I already spent all my money," Beth said.

"I know."

"Here," the guy said, lifting the necklace from the stand and handing it to Beth. With Sophie's help, she fastened it around her neck.

"It's not gold," I said.

She reached for the mirror, tilting it so she could see.

"Don't you want to say 'thank you' to your sister?" Sophie asked.

Beth threw her arms around me and said, "Thank you, thank you, thank you. It's *beautiful*." Then she stepped back and examined her reflection. Raising her eyebrows, she put her hands on her hips and cocked one shoulder forward. "Really?" she mouthed to an imaginary admirer. "You do?"

I caught Sophie's eye and smiled.

24

ON SATURDAY, Ariel called and asked if I wanted to come to her house that afternoon instead of meeting at Java Jive's.

"You know, to report on our dreams," she said. She paused, then added, "I made a Tunnel of Fudge."

"A what?" I said.

"A Tunnel of Fudge. It's this awesome cake from the Pillsbury Bake-Off Contest."

"Oh," I said. Still, for an instant I balked, feeling that old sense of being backed into something. Coffeehouses were safer: there were other people around, it was neutral territory. But then I realized—and it was weird that I had to *realize*, that I didn't just know—that I liked Ariel. As I drove to her house, I remembered all the judgments I'd made about her, and I felt bad, because wasn't that exactly what was so messed up about Kate? The way she focused only on how things looked on the surface, instead of pushing deeper and figuring things out for herself?

I pulled into Ariel's drive and cut the motor. For several seconds I sat there, listening to the engine pop, and then I unbuckled my seat belt and stepped outside. A flutter of cloth in the kitchen window caught my eye, and I saw Ariel holding back the curtain and waving. The curtain dropped, and she came out the front door to greet me.

"Lissa! Hey!" she called. "I thought maybe you'd changed your mind."

"What? No way." I took a step forward. "Nice house."

"Yeah?" She glanced up the street at the other, almost identical houses and made a face that suggested she wasn't so sure. "Come on in. I'll get you some cake."

The kitchen was bright and sunny and very clean. A spice rack on the counter held alphabetized jars of spices, and matching blue and pink pot holders hung from the cabinet knobs to the left of the oven. Above the sink hung a framed piece of needlepoint that said "Bless This Mess."

Ariel grabbed two plates from the cabinet and cut into a chocolate bundt cake with drizzly chocolate frosting.

"Yay, yay, yay," she said, lightly clapping her hands as she examined the inside of the cake. "Sometimes the tunnel part collapses, and it becomes an avalanche of fudge instead. It tastes good either way, but I'm so glad it turned out."

She handed me my plate and watched as I took a bite. The outer edge of the cake was rich and moist, while the inside, as promised, tasted like a dense ribbon of gooey fudge. "Mmm," I said. "You are a goddess."

The screen door squeaked, and Ariel's mom came in loaded with shopping bags from Neiman Marcus and Saks Fifth Avenue. Behind her trailed a girl a year or two younger than Ariel and me.

"Hi, girls," Mrs. Thomas said. She put her bags on the table and pushed back her hair. "You must be Lissa. Nice to meet you."

"Nice to meet you, too."

"That's Shannon," Ariel said, nodding at her sister.

"Hi," I said.

Shannon leaned against the counter. She was small and blond and looked bored. "No nose ring?" she said to me.

"What?"

She walked over and scooped a dab of frosting from the cake plate. Ariel snatched the cake and moved it.

"Mom," Shannon said, "tell Kimberly she has to let me have some."

For a second the name threw me, and then I remembered: Kimberly/Ariel; Ariel/Kimberly.

"I'm sure Kimberly will be happy to share," Mrs. Thomas said.

I shifted my weight. It was strange that Shannon and Mrs. Thomas still called Ariel "Kimberly." Or maybe Ariel hadn't told them she'd changed it? I'd thought of her as Ariel for so long that Kimberly now sounded wrong.

Ariel glared at Shannon, then opened the refrigerator and poured two glasses of milk. She handed one to me and said, "Come on. Let's go to my room."

"Watch for crumbs," Mrs. Thomas called. "And please bring back your dishes!"

Upstairs, I settled myself on Ariel's floor and broke off a piece of cake. I thought about Ariel's mom, how she was pretty in a tired sort of way. And Shannon was a pain, but what little sister wasn't every so often? Mainly, they both just seemed normal. I looked at Ariel and smiled.

"What?" she said.

"Nothing. I like your room." My eyes traveled from her colorful bedspread to the Mardi Gras beads draped over the side of her mirror. I *did* like her room, although it, too, was more normal than I'd have guessed. But what did I expect? Black walls? Shrines to Inanna piled with tea cakes and dowsing rods?

"So," Ariel said, "I tried those techniques you told me about, but I haven't had a lucid dream yet. What about you? Any luck?"

I leaned back against the wall. I hadn't had a lucid dream this entire week, not one. I felt as if I'd stalled out. It frustrated me.

"None," I said.

"I almost had one, I think. I was having a dream about being at the grocery store, only for some reason I had all this gunk in my mouth. Like wet sand. It was disgusting. And I kept spitting it out and spitting it out, and I remember thinking, 'God, this can't be real. I *have* to be dreaming.' But even though I thought that, it didn't shoot me into a lucid dream."

"Weird," I said.

"I think the gunky stuff was my mouth guard," she said. She blushed and rolled her eyes. "I wear a mouth guard when I go to bed. Isn't that gross?"

"You mean, like a retainer?"

"Sort of. It's like what football players wear, only smaller. It's to keep me from grinding my teeth."

I envisioned Ariel in bed, her heavy eyeliner gone and her mouth guard in place. "It's not gross."

She pulled her legs up to her chest and rested her cheek on

her knee. She was quiet for a moment, then said, "I really wanted to have one, though. A lucid dream."

"Yeah."

"Sometimes I just . . . I don't know. It would just be so nice to have something special happen, you know?"

Her expression was so wistful that it felt wrong not to tell her. I put down my plate. "Um . . . actually, I *did* have a lucid dream. Not this week, but a while ago. Before we even talked about it."

She lifted her head. "You did?"

I swallowed. "Two of them."

"Lissa!" She sat straight up. "So *tell* me about them. Tell me, tell me, tell me!"

She didn't ask why I hadn't told her before, and I was glad. I told her about my moon dream and then about my weird floating dream, how I imagined myself drifting around the house like a ghost. She listened with parted lips, and when I came to the part about bumping up against the window, she laughed and slapped the floor.

"That is so strange," she said. "And cool. So then what?"

"Well, I finally floated outside, and it was all dark and kind of spooky. And I looked down, and below me was—"

I stopped. Ariel lifted her eyebrows.

"A girl," I said. "Just this girl, walking on the street. And then the dream shifted, and I was in my bathroom flossing my teeth. Isn't that bizarre?" I spoke quickly, scrunching my toes in my sneakers.

"Wow," Ariel said.

"Yeah. Although what was *really* weird was how real it felt. Even though I knew I was dreaming."

Ariel shook her head. "Isn't it amazing the stuff we can convince ourselves of? And not just in our dreams, but in our normal lives, too. You know?"

I wondered what she was thinking of, what lies she'd convinced herself were truths. But I didn't ask.

I stayed at Ariel's for a couple of hours. We agreed to keep working on having lucid dreams, and I gave her more tips, such as memorizing certain dream signals (for her, maybe the gunk-in-the-mouth thing) and telling herself that the next time that happens, she *will* realize she's dreaming. I hoped that by talking about it, maybe I'd get things back on track for me as well.

At 5:30, we headed over to Darlin's, me in my truck and Ariel in her Volvo. I had to be home by 7:00 to meet Finn, but I figured there was no reason I couldn't deliver an order or two. It would give me something to do.

But Darlin had other plans. She ushered Ariel and me into the living room, sat us down, and brought out a bottle of sparkling cider. "A toast," she said, untwisting the wire cap. She filled our glasses and beamed at us.

"What?" Ariel said, looking from Darlin to me. I lifted my eyebrows, and she turned back to Darlin. "Darlin, what's going on?"

"To *Darlin's Delights*," she said, clinking her glass against ours. "Or maybe that's too cute. *Darlin's Delicacies*? Or just plain *Darlin's*?"

"What are you talking about?" Ariel demanded.

"I've decided to do it," Darlin said. "I'm going to phase out Entrées on Trays—"

"What? Why?!"

"—and start my own catering business. My *own* catering business, with my food and my recipes. And hopefully a ready-made list of clients, if only they'll trust me to cook for them!"

"Oh, Darlin, they will!" Ariel said. "They totally will!" She put down her cider and gave Darlin a hug. "Darlin, that's awesome!"

"Yeah," I said. "That's great!"

"And you two will be my charming and courteous servers, of course. If you want to be. I'll run it by my weekday drivers, too, and see who all is interested. I've got so much to do—apply for a business license, update my kitchen, create a menu—but I'm enjoying every minute of it. Can I tell you how wonderful that feels?"

"It's because you're doing what you love," Ariel said. "You're following your heart."

"Oh, girls," Darlin said, squeezing us both. "My soul is in a riotous condition. It's the truth. But if I start with this . . . well, we'll just see, won't we?"

Ariel and I celebrated with Darlin for a little over half an hour, until at 6:15 I glanced at my watch and made a face.

"Shit," I said. "I've got to get going."

"Ooo, that's right," Ariel said. To Darlin she announced, "Lissa's got a date."

"A date?" Darlin repeated. She looked surprised.

"She's going out for pizza with this awesome guy named Finn," Ariel said. A line formed between her eyebrows, but disappeared when she smiled. "It's very exciting."

"It really isn't," I said. "It's just that I'm never going to make it if—"

"Yeah, yeah, yeah," Ariel said. She walked me to the door, then waved as I hurried to my truck. "Have fun! Don't do anything I wouldn't do!"

I glanced back, ready to make some smart remark, and saw that Darlin had joined Ariel in the doorway.

"Just remember to follow your heart," Darlin said. She said it lightly, but her gaze was steady. "Take care of yourself, baby."

My retort dried up, and I turned away.

25

I STOOD IN MY BATHROBE before the mirror. My skin was flushed from my shower, and I liked the way my hair looked when it was wet. Fuller, darker, and sticking up in interesting clumps when I raked my fingers through it. It was getting longer, too. My bangs grazed my eyebrows now, and the sides had finally grown out enough to shove behind my ears. I spied Beth's mousse behind a bottle of lotion and pulled it out, weighing it in my hand. What the hell. I squirted an egg-sized pouf into my palm and smeared it into my hair. There— maybe now it would stay the way I wanted it.

In my room, I slipped on my new shirt and a pair of faded jeans that hung low on my hips. I was fishing under my bed for my brown leather belt when the telephone rang. "Dammit," I muttered. I scooted backward and reached for the phone. "Hello?"

"Lissa, hi," Kate said.

My heart skipped a beat. "Hi. What's up?"

"Nothing much. Dad's grilling some chicken and Mom's complaining, as usual. Says he's got the temperature too high, that the outside will be roasted before the inside has a chance to cook." She snorted. "Now she's saying we'll all get salmonella and die in our chairs. Can you hear her?"

I laughed. "Just barely."

"What about you? Getting ready for your big date?" She said it in a teasing way, as if she didn't really care, but I knew she did. Otherwise, why would she call?

"Finn's going to be here in ten minutes," I said. "But I can't find my leather belt."

"The one with the silver buckle?"

"Uh-huh."

"You can borrow mine, if you want. I could bring it over."

"That's okay," I said. "I'll figure something out." I did *not* want Kate here when Finn picked me up. It would be too weird.

"Well, have fun," she said. "That's all I called to say."

"Okay. Uh, thanks. What are you going to do tonight?"

"I don't know. Sit around, watch movies. *Vertigo* is on at ten o'clock."

"I love that movie."

"So come over and watch it. Blow Finn off." Again that teasing tone, and when I didn't answer, she said, "I'm kidding. You know I'm kidding, right?"

"I've got to go. I've got to finish getting dressed."

"Yeah, well, dinner's ready, so I've got to go, too. Wish me luck."

"I'm sure you'll survive."

"Yeah," she said. She paused. "You, too."

"Man," Finn said, sitting across from me with his forearms on the table. "I am really hungry."

"Me, too," I said.

"Our pizza should get here soon."

"Hope so. They usually don't take too long."

We looked at each other, then looked away. This most recent exchange was one of several conversational dead ends we'd run into this evening. On the ride over we'd given in-depth coverage to the weather. Chillier than usual for this time of year, don't you think? Yep, sure is chilly. And when we arrived at the restaurant, we had a brief flurry of conversation over what kind of pizza to order. Other than that, we'd both been as interesting as doorknobs.

"How about them Braves?" Finn threw out.

I raised my eyebrows. "How 'bout 'em?"

"One large pepperoni and sausage," our waiter announced, descending upon us with a golden-brown pizza. "Watch out, it's hot. Anything else you need?"

"No, thanks," Finn said. "We're fine."

I served Finn and then myself, and we went at it like we were starving. "Ow," I said, fanning my tongue after burning it with the sauce.

"But good, huh?"

"Mmm. Delicious."

We smiled at each other.

"So did you hang out with Ariel today?" he asked. "Talk about dreams?"

He said it with a lilt, and I felt a stab of defensiveness. But then I remembered what Ariel said, about how Finn acted all mocking on the outside but was really just shy. He was probably just trying to find something to talk about.

"We did," I said. "It was fun."

"I bet. Ariel's all fired up to unravel the mysteries of her subconscious, which, of course, is a huge load of psycho-babble. You don't really believe that stuff, do you? That dreams are the windows to our souls?"

"I never said I did."

"Then why bother analyzing them to death?"

I stirred my Sprite with my straw. I let the straw go, and it kept spinning on its own. "I don't know," I said. "Even if dreams aren't the windows to our souls, even if they're just these random things, we still wake up thinking about them."

"So?"

"So whatever meaning we give them is just as revealing as the dream itself. Maybe more so. It's like that test with the ink blots. What's that called? Where it says one thing about you if you think the blot is a flower, and something totally different if you think it's, I don't know, a spider or something?"

Finn looked dubious.

"Come on," I said. "Haven't you had dreams that felt really important for some reason? And by trying to figure them out, you figured out something about yourself?"

"No."

"Seriously?"

He tore off a piece of his crust. "Look. I'm not saying it's *bad* that you believe in that stuff. I'm just surprised. I guess I saw you as more skeptical, that's all."

I opened my mouth to answer, then closed it. I guess I saw me as more skeptical, too. At least I used to.

"I don't know," I said. "There's so much in the world I can't even begin to understand. So many possibilities. I don't want to rule anything out."

Finn held my gaze, then slowly nodded.

Later, when he walked me to my door, he tried to kiss me. He leaned forward, very gentle, but I felt his breath on my lips and pulled away. He blushed and wrapped his arms around his chest, hiding his hands beneath his armpits.

"No," I said, "it's not—"

"It's all right. I understand."

"Finn, wait. I really like you. I think you're great."

"But you just want to be friends." He turned toward me, daring me to disagree.

My face got hot. "It's not . . . it's not what you—"

"Yeah, well, it never is." He got in his car and turned on the motor. "See you around."

I waited until his tail lights were no longer visible, then reached into my pocket and pulled out my keys. But I didn't go inside. I climbed into my truck and drove to Kate's, as perhaps I'd known all along I would.

26

"OH, NO," KATE SAID. She giggled. "The weather? You talked about the weather?"

"For, like, fifteen minutes at least. We decided conclusively that it was cold out—which, interestingly enough, we already knew, since the heater in his car didn't work and we shivered all the way to the restaurant. Smiled and shivered and talked about the damn weather."

Kate hid her head in her hands. She was already in her pajamas, and I'd had to toss pebbles at her window to get her to let me in. We'd tiptoed to the kitchen, where she snagged some Oreos from her dad's hidden stash, and then we'd padded upstairs to her room.

I grabbed a cookie and leaned against the side of her bed. "It wasn't all bad, though. I mean, he's really a nice guy. Once we got to Fellini's, things got better."

"Well, that's good."

"And the pizza was great. Sausage and pepperoni."

"So you got a good meal out of it, anyway." She glanced at my face and said, "Just kidding. That was mean."

I twisted open the Oreo and balanced the two halves on my knee. "He tried to kiss me."

Alarm flicked in her eyes, although I wouldn't have noticed if I hadn't been watching for it.

"Oh, yeah?" she said.

"Afterward, when he dropped me off."

"Huh."

"I didn't let him."

She wet her lips. "Why not?"

My heart thumped, but I didn't back down. "Because I didn't want to. Because if there's anyone I wanted to kiss—"

She stiffened.

"—it would be you." The split-open Oreo was still on my knee, the cookie-half next to the icing-half. A wink. And as I stared at it, something inside of me shifted and came dislodged. "I'm sorry," I said, "but it would. And I'm not going to pretend everything's normal again just because you can't deal with it."

"Excuse me?" she said. Her cheeks flamed with color. "I can't deal with it? I'm the one who called you, I'm the one who came up to you after we fought—"

"Yeah, and you'll talk about anything but that night, anything but what actually happened. And if I happen to stand too close, God forbid, you pull back like I've got rabies or something!"

She glanced at the door. "Lissa—"

"What? You're worried your parents will hear us?" I lowered

my voice, while at the same time hating myself for doing it. "All you care about is what people might think. And I do, too. Of course I do. But what we have . . . what we did . . . I'm not giving it up just because it's not *normal*, whatever that is."

Kate looked like she was about to cry. I stared at my lap, at the stupid Oreo balanced on my thigh, and brushed the two halves to the floor.

"I wish you could just forget about it," she said. "Why can't you forget it ever happened?"

"Because it *did* happen, and it was wonderful. At least until Rob and Ben showed up." I took a breath. "I don't . . . I'm not trying to make things hard. It's just . . . God, Kate. You're the most incredible person I've ever known."

She plucked at her pajamas. She didn't speak for several seconds, and when she did, her voice was barely audible. "I broke up with Ben," she whispered.

"What?"

"It was me, not him."

I remembered how he looked that day by her locker, how desperate he was for her attention. "What are you saying?"

"He didn't fool around with Alice Spradling at Terri's party. I made that up."

"Then why did you . . ."

"I don't *know*. I just did." She drew her knees to her chest. "Because when he kissed me . . ."

My mouth went dry.

"You already know," she said. She wiped at her eyes. "God. Why am I being like this? Why am I acting like such an idiot? It's just that this stuff between us . . . It scares me, Lissa."

"It scares me, too. But we can't just ignore it."

"We can't?" She lifted her head and kind of laughed. I didn't. She stopped smiling, and when she spoke, she spoke to the floor. "Ben's a nice guy, but when he kissed me, nothing happened. Okay?"

I gazed at her. In the past, Kate had been the confident one. The leader. This time, I led the way. I leaned over and touched her face. I kissed her, and her lips opened against mine. She tasted like icing, like a summer night and a swirl of bright color.

And then her hand was on my shoulder, pushing me away. "Don't," she whispered.

I didn't listen.

"*Don't!*"

"Kate—" I touched her leg, and she tensed up. "But you said—"

"I can't. I just . . . I can't."

"Kate, why are you being this way? You said you felt it, too. You said that. And if it's what we both want—"

"It's *not* what I want." She lifted her head. "I'm not like you, Lissa. I'm not a fucking dyke, all right?"

I drew back as if I'd been slapped.

"I didn't mean that," she said quickly. "It's just . . . why do you have to argue with me all the time?" She raked her hand through her hair. "God. Just because I don't want to kiss you—why does that have to change everything?"

Tears burned in my eyes as I got to my feet. My face scrunched up and a sound came out of my throat, but even then I didn't leave. I stood there, waiting for her to stop me, and only when she looked away did I realize she already had.

CHAPTER

27

THAT NIGHT I DREAMED that Kate leaned over in the middle of history class and whispered that we should both take our shirts off, that it would be fun. I went along with it, but as soon as I pulled off my shirt, the entire class started laughing.

"It was a *joke*," Kate said.

I woke up with puffy eyes. I drew my quilt around my shoulders and tried to push everything out of my mind, but my fight with Kate kept playing in my head. And what destroyed me, what made me feel raw with shame, was that the things Kate said—that she wanted only friendship, that she wasn't "like" me—were the same things she'd been saying ever since that night at the gazebo. I just hadn't wanted to listen.

I kicked off the covers and sat up, squinting against the light. My clock said 11:33 A.M. Was that possible?

I put my feet on the cold wooden floor. My body felt shaky, and I almost crawled back beneath the sheets. But I didn't, because beneath the hurt and embarrassment, there was a small place inside of me that said no. I thought of Darlin, .how she'd taken charge of her life when things had gotten hard, and my resolve strengthened. I had to move on.

I grabbed my school directory from the drawer of my nightstand and flipped through the pages until I came to *Kimberly Thomas*. Before I could change my mind, I took a breath and punched in the numbers.

"Hello?" Ariel said after the second ring.

"Hi," I said. "It's Lissa."

"Hey! What's up?" She sounded glad to hear from me.

"Nothing much. I was . . . I was wondering if you might want to hang out or something. Go get some coffee."

"Sure. When?"

"Uh . . ."

"Now?"

I nodded, then realized that she couldn't see that over the phone. "That'd be great. Java Jive's?"

"Sounds good. And you can tell me about your date with Finn."

I closed my eyes. Until this minute, I'd honestly forgotten about that part of the night. But it was all part of the same thing, and that's why I was calling Ariel in the first place. "Yeah, I'll tell you everything."

Ariel listened while I told her about dinner with Finn. She stirred her mocha latte and spooned swirls of whipped cream to her lips, and when I got to the part about Finn kissing me, she paused with the spoon still in her mouth. "He did?" she said. She looked a little stunned, but then she took out the spoon and tried again. "He kissed you? That's awesome!"

"Wait," I said. "I pulled away."

"Why?"

"I'm not attracted to him, not like that." I fiddled with the napkin dispenser, then set it down. I stared at my hands. "The thing is . . . well, the reason I called you . . . Shit. It's not even that big a deal. I mean, it *is*, but . . ."

"What?" Ariel said.

I held myself still. "I think . . . I might be gay."

She laughed. "Because you didn't want to kiss Finn? Poor guy. I don't think he's heard that one before." She stopped laughing when I didn't join in. She touched my arm. "Lissa?"

"I'm not joking."

She studied me. "Kate?" she said at last.

I nodded.

"Does she know?"

"She knows. And she doesn't—" My throat closed, and my shoulders started to shake.

Ariel's hand tightened on my forearm, and then she scooted from her side of the booth to mine. She put her arm around me. I would have thought my tears were all used up, but clearly they weren't.

"Kate's really stupid," Ariel said softly, "if she's willing to give you up."

"You don't think it's weird? Abnormal?"

"What, that you like a girl? I think *you're* weird and maybe a little abnormal, but not because of that."

I reached for a napkin and blew my nose. "Great. Thanks."

"I like weird," she said. "But Lissa . . ."

I crumpled the napkin in my palm.

"Just because you're into Kate . . . well, it doesn't necessarily mean you're gay. Although it's okay if you are. But if that's what's worrying you . . ." She sighed. "God. It shouldn't be so hard to talk about this stuff. All I'm saying is maybe you're gay or maybe you're not. Maybe you're bi. Or maybe it's totally a Kate thing. Maybe you'd want to be with her whether she was a girl *or* a boy."

I blinked. I didn't know if what she said made things better or worse.

"Have you liked other girls?" she asked.

"No."

"Well, see?"

"Yeah, but Ariel . . ." I pushed myself up so that I was no longer leaning against her. "There was this party. And Kate and I both got a little drunk . . . Well, *she* did. I didn't. And . . . I don't know. Things happened. And for the longest time, I tried to tell myself that it didn't mean anything, but it did. It *does*. And I'm sick of shoving those feelings away."

A funny expression crossed Ariel's face.

"What?" I said.

"Nothing. I just . . . I know what you mean."

"You do?"

"Well, yeah. Kind of. Although it's nothing compared to what you're dealing with." She gnawed on her thumbnail. "It's just that I'm not, like, totally depressed that things didn't work out between you and Finn."

"Huh?"

"Like I said, it's nothing like what you're going through. But when I said how excited I was for you two . . ."

It took me a second, and then I shook my head. "But I asked you, back when we first started hanging out. You said you were just friends."

"I know. Pitiful, huh?"

I gazed at her, then half-laughed and half-sniffled. "God, aren't we?"

A man frowned at us as he made his way to one of the few remaining tables, and I grew aware of our half-finished drinks, which had grown cold. Aware, too, of how close we were sitting.

"Can we get out of here?" I said.

"Of course," Ariel said. "We could go to my house, if you want, or we could go to the park. Want to go to the park?"

She linked her arm through mine as we headed for the door. I felt sure that everyone was watching, but I didn't pull away.

CHAPTER

28

I SAW KATE EVERY DAY in history, of course. She returned to sitting with Missy Colquitt, and I returned to sitting alone at the back of the class. On Thursday, Mr. Neilson asked her to distribute some work sheets, and she slid out from behind her desk and strolled to the front of the room. She wore soft black corduroys and a cranberry-colored sweater, and her hair was held off her neck with a thick silver clip. Mitch Kremer leaned forward and whispered something as she moved down our row, and she smiled and swatted him with the stack of handouts. When she got to me, she dropped her eyes. She placed a handout on my desk and moved on.

That night I went home and thought about how stupid it was that we were ignoring each other again. I was still angry, and hurt, but pretending that she didn't exist didn't help.

So on Friday, I got to class early and walked to her desk like it was the most natural thing in the world. "Hi, Kate," I said. I held my books tight against my chest.

"Hi," she said. Her hand went to her earring, and she pushed the hook in and out of her ear. "Um, how are you?"

"I'm okay. You?"

She let her hand fall to her desk, and she glanced around the room. Missy had arrived and taken her seat, and most of the other kids had straggled in as well. "Great," she said. "I'm great." She smiled as if to say *why wouldn't I be?* and I knew she was playing to an audience, even if she wasn't aware of it.

"Oh," she said, widening her eyes as if something had just occurred to her. "I totally need your help with last night's homework, because there were a couple of answers I couldn't find. I mean, God, you're a thousand times better at this stuff than I am."

I almost got sucked in. It would have been so easy. But feeling needed was one thing; having your own needs met was another.

"They're in the handout," I told her. "You just have to look."

She stopped digging in her backpack and lifted her head.

I hugged my arms closer around my books. "See you around."

That afternoon, Ariel and I drove to a bookstore in Little Five Points called Charis. Ariel had a cousin who worked there, a cousin who happened to be gay.

"This isn't a setup, is it?" I asked. "Because you already tried that."

"It's not a setup," Ariel assured me. "It's just . . . why not, you know? Maybe you can talk to her about stuff."

"Oh, right. Like I can ask her if her best friend ever came on to her and then rejected her all in the same month, stuff like that."

"If you want," she said, refusing to be baited.

I took a right on Highland Avenue. "How'd you find out she was gay?"

Ariel propped her feet on the dashboard. "It was at her twenty-first birthday party. We were having a fancy family dinner in her honor, and my aunt kept making these stupid remarks about marriage and babies and biological clocks. Tick-tick-tick, that kind of thing. So Jessica took me and Shannon up to her room and told us what a crock it was. And she told us that Taylor, her roommate, was really her girl-friend."

"Are you close, you and Jessica? I mean, that's a big thing to tell someone."

"Pretty close."

"So what'd you say?"

"I said I thought it was great. Shannon thought it was gross. But that's Shannon for you."

I kept my eyes on the road. "Kate called me a dyke. Actually, she called me a 'fucking dyke,' which, now that I think about it, I'm not sure is possible."

Ariel snorted. She draped her arm out of the open window and flexed her fingers to catch the breeze. "She was just scared. Most people have no idea how to handle anything that's dif-ferent. You know that."

"Yeah, I guess." I thought of Ariel's dream, how she saw herself standing alone at the bottom of the world. "Doesn't it ever get to you? The kids at school, how they . . ."

"Treat me like a freak? No." She frowned. "Well, maybe. Sometimes. But I just remind myself that this is high school. It's not forever."

That was true. Next year we'd be seniors. I glanced at her as she raked her hand through her hair, making it stand up in orange spikes. It struck me that being a senior with Ariel didn't sound so bad.

We found a parking space behind a vegetarian restaurant, then walked a couple of blocks until we came to a small store with a pink awning. A few feet from the door, I asked Ariel one last question. "What about Finn? Have you told him you like him?"

"Not exactly." A flush crept up her face, and she paused in front of the stucco storefront. "But yesterday we studied together up in my room, and I got him to paint my toenails. And then I painted his, and I told him what nice feet he had. You think that's a big enough hint?"

"He let you paint his toenails?"

A smile tugged at her mouth. "It took some persuading."

I grinned. "I'd say you're there, Ariel. Way to go."

We went into the store, and from behind the cash register a woman with long curly hair lifted her head. "Hey!" she said. She came over and gave Ariel a hug. She turned to me and stuck out her hand. "Hi, I'm Jessica. You must be Lissa."

"Hi," I said.

"You want some tea? Hot chocolate?" She scanned the empty store. "We've got the place to ourselves, so we can pretty much do what we want."

"Hot chocolate would be great," Ariel said.

"Sure," I said. "Thanks." I'd been worried that I'd feel

strange around Jessica, like maybe I was being sized up. I'd
also worried that she'd be wearing combat boots or a sleeve-
less undershirt, but she looked perfectly normal. She had dark
brown eyes and a round, smiley face, and on the front of her
shirt was the logo for Mr. Bubble.

"I'll stick some water in the microwave," she said, "and I'll
call Taylor and tell her to come over. How long has it been
since she's seen you?"

"I don't know," Ariel said. "Shannon's birthday party?"

"That's right. How is Shannon?"

Ariel rolled her eyes. "The same. Yesterday at dinner I was
complaining about how the cheerleaders cheer for the boys'
teams but not the girls', and she told me I was anti-American.
She said I should just move to Germany if that's the way
I felt."

Jessica laughed and ducked to the back of the store.

"She seems nice," I said.

"Yeah. Thank God there's someone sane in my family."

Taylor arrived as Jessica was serving us our hot chocolate,
and the four of us leaned against the front counter and talked
about books and music and what movies we'd recently seen.
Sometimes, while Ariel chattered away, I studied Jessica and
Taylor from under my bangs. I liked how affectionate they
were with each other: the way Taylor smiled and nodded
when Jessica said something funny, and the way Jessica found
Taylor's hand on the countertop, covering it with her own.

At one point a customer came in, and when Jessica slipped
away to help her find a book, Taylor told Ariel and me about
a ceramics class Jessica was taking. "She's too modest to bring
it up," Taylor said, "but you should see the pieces she's been

glazing. She uses blues and greens and golds, mainly, and even though the designs are different, all of the pieces look good together."

"That's so cool," Ariel said. Her eyes were bright, and I could tell she was taken by the idea of the artist's life.

"Planning your next career?" I teased.

"Maybe. I could do it!"

We hung out for another half hour, and then Ariel pushed herself up from the counter and announced that we should go.

"It was good seeing you," Ariel told Taylor. She poked Jessica's shoulder. "And you need to show me some of your pottery the next time you come over. Okay?"

"Taylor—" Jessica said.

"What?" Taylor said. "I'm not allowed to brag?"

Jessica's cheeks turned pink, but I could tell she was pleased. "You should come by more often," she said to Ariel. She turned to me. "You, too, Lissa." She held my gaze. "Ariel told me a little about what you're going through—just a little—and if you ever need someone to talk to . . ."

I could sense Ariel beside me, holding her breath.

"Thanks," I said. "I will."

CHAPTER

29

SATURDAY MORNING DAWNED bright and sunny. I kicked off the covers, but stayed in bed, stretching my arms above my head.

"Lissa?" Beth called. She knocked on my door. "You awake?"

I yawned.

She came in and perched on the edge of the mattress. She was wearing her new necklace, along with two purple barrettes.

"Nice barrettes," I said.

"Do they match?"

"They do. You are the fashion queen."

She craned her neck to look at herself in the mirror over my dresser, then turned back to me. "So. Jerry and Sophie are taking Nikki and me to the zoo because it's such a nice day out, and you know they have baby koalas now."

"Who, Jerry and Sophie?"

"The *zoo*. But you can only see them once a day when the zoo people feed them, because they're nocturnal."

"The zoo people are nocturnal?"

"Lissa! Do you want to come or not?"

"Sounds fun, but Ariel's coming over at eleven o'clock. Say 'hi' to Nikki for me, though."

"Okay." She got up from the bed.

"Hey," I said.

She turned around.

"What about Vanessa?"

"What about her?" She lifted her eyebrows, then spun on her heel and strode out the door.

"*So*," Ariel said. She grabbed my hands and pulled me into the den, then sat next to me on the sofa and bounced up and down. "Guess who just happened to kiss me last night?"

"No way!" I said.

"Way! Although technically *I* kissed him, but he didn't seem all that upset about it."

"Ariel, that's awesome," I said. I felt only a ping of jealousy. It was just that I wanted that for myself one day: to be into someone and have whoever it was be into me, too. "So what did he say? Was he surprised?"

"Not as much as you might think. I mean, there we were watching the movie, and then wham! I was all over him." She grinned. "But then he told me he'd wanted to do the same thing ages ago. It's just that we'd been friends for so long, and he didn't want to mess things up." She flung herself onto the cushions. "God, what a beautiful boy."

I smiled. I was glad she was happy, but I couldn't help thinking that only a week ago, Finn had tried to kiss me. Was that a bad sign, that he could go from one person to the next in such a short time? Then again, I'd done pretty much the same thing by fleeing to Kate on the very night he'd taken me out to dinner. Oh, well. So we both had someone else in mind when we tried each other out. Was that really such a crime?

A lightness filled my chest as I realized that I could think about this—about Kate—and not fall to pieces.

"What about you?" Ariel said. She nudged my leg with her foot. "You seem like you're in a good mood, too."

I turned toward her, bringing myself back to the moment. "As a matter of fact, I am." I paused. "I had another lucid dream last night."

"Lissa! You stud! I've been trying and trying, and I still haven't had one. So tell me about it!"

"Well, it was weird. But wonderful, too." I leaned into the sofa. "First I had this icky dream—not a lucid dream, just a normal dream. It was a dream I used to have a lot, even way back when I was a kid. But for a while I hadn't had it, and I'd hoped it was gone."

Ariel seemed confused.

"I know," I said. "It's kind of complicated." I backtracked and told her what had happened when I was five, how I was supposed to be waiting for Mom outside Service Merchandise, but instead I almost got myself kidnapped.

"And for years I had these awful dreams about it," I said, "which I guess isn't so surprising. And then for a while the dreams went away. But in the last few weeks that same dream came back, and it got mixed up with other stuff, too. Like one time Ben Porter and Rob Lynch were in it, leaning against a car and laughing at me."

"Yuck," Ariel said.

"And another time I dreamed about a kid from my elementary school, this girl named Cookie Churchill. She was, like, luring me farther into the parking lot."

"*Cookie*?" Ariel said.

"Yeah. We used to be friends, sort of, but sometimes she'd be mean to me, too. Like if I got upset about something, she'd say, 'What's your prob, little snob?' And one time she told the whole class my toenails were gross."

"So why'd you hang out with her?"

"I don't know. I honestly don't." I shrugged. "I guess I still liked her, even though she made me feel like crap."

Ariel looked at me in an odd way.

"What?" I said.

"You heard what you just said, right?" She waited, then raised her eyebrows. "You still liked her, even though she made you feel like crap?"

"Yeah, well, I was in third grade. Give me a break."

"That's not what I mean," she said. "Cookie doesn't remind you of anyone? Someone who *isn't* in third grade?"

"Ariel, I have no idea what you're—" I stopped. Blood rushed to my face. "Oh. Oh, God, I didn't think about it like that."

"In your dream it was Cookie, but I bet it was really Kate."

"Wow, that is so weird," I said. I thought about it for a second. "But yeah, they both treated me the same, didn't they? That kind of freaks me out."

"Tell me about it," Ariel said. "I had a dream like that about Mickey Mouse, when actually it was my dad." She leaned forward. "Okay, so keep going. What ended up happening?"

"Well, last night I had the dream *again*," I said, "and when I woke up, I just got mad. Because why should I keep having a dream that makes me feel so awful?"

"You shouldn't," Ariel said.

"Exactly. And then I thought about this chapter from my dream book, how the author says you can re-enter a dream on purpose and turn it into a lucid dream. You're supposed to think about the dream as you slip back to sleep, telling yourself that the next time you have it, you'll realize you're just dreaming. And then you can deal with it however you want. *You* control the dream, instead of the other way around."

I checked her expression. I felt jumpy, but I wanted to make sure she was getting it. "So that's what I did," I said. "And it worked."

"Are you serious? Lissa, that's amazing!"

"It really kind of was," I said. I drew my legs up on the sofa, folding them beneath me. "I closed my eyes and let myself drift off, thinking about the dream the entire time. And then there I was, standing in the middle of the parking lot. The same parking lot as all the times before. And it was hot, and the sky was blue, and I had that creepy feeling on the back of my neck, you know? Like something terrible was going to happen."

"Because something terrible *was* going to happen," Ariel said. She shivered. "That is so spooky, Lissa, that you really did walk off with that guy."

I pushed my hair behind my ear. "So . . . I was in the parking lot, and all the cars were, like, really bright. I can't even describe it, just that they weren't like regular cars. And I was standing there, feeling all edgy and wondering what I was supposed to do, when someone called my name."

"Ooo. Was it Cookie, who was really Kate?" She slapped her knee, a series of excited pats. "That would make sense, wouldn't it? That instead of, like, this dangerous guy, you were being drawn toward the whole Kate situation?"

"Maybe," I said. "Except whoever it was called out from behind me, not in front of me. And at first I told myself, *No, you can't turn back now. You've got to go forward, you've got to face whatever it is you're so afraid of.*"

"You are so brave," Ariel said.

"Yeah, well, but then I heard the voice again."

Ariel frowned. She looped a strand of hair around her finger. Then her eyes widened and she asked, "Was it. . . your mom?" She said it gingerly, as if afraid of overstepping.

"For a second I thought so, too. But it wasn't."

"So who was it?"

I swallowed. I remembered how my heart, in my dream, had started pounding like crazy when at last I turned around. "It was me," I said. "Me when I was five, with my hair in two long braids." I tucked my legs in closer. "I was standing outside the store, and I was safe after all."

"Oh, wow," Ariel said.

"Yeah," I said. I suddenly felt embarrassed. "And then I woke up. And I knew things were going to be okay."

She gazed at me in this proud way. A little teary, even. "So the scary stuff *was* Kate," she said. "Kate and Ben and—I don't know. Even me, I guess, pressuring you to be someone you

197

weren't. *That's* the horrible fate you've been marching off toward all this time, even though deep inside you knew you shouldn't."

I stared at my jeans.

"But you called yourself back," she said. "You called yourself back, and you were finally able to listen."

My throat tightened, and my lower lip got that trembly feeling of wanting to cry. I thought about Mom, who used to stand behind me and fix my hair. *Like corn silk,* she would say, weaving the sections with her fingers. How long had it been since I'd thought of that?

Ariel put her arm around me, and I leaned into her embrace.